I0451771

Shadow's Moon

Ash Rock Series
Marcelle Valentine

 Medusa Publishing

Shadow's Moon Season One
Ash Rock Series
Copyright © 2022 By Marcelle Valentine

All rights reserved. No part of this book can be used, reproduced, transmitted, or distributed without written consent from the author, except for instances where a brief quotation is being used in an article or review.

This book is a work of fiction. Unless otherwise indicated, any and all of the names, characters, businesses, places, events, and incidents in this book are either the product of the author's imagination or used in a fictitious manner. Any resemblance to a real location, persons living or dead, or actual events is purely coincidental.

Contact information: marcellevalentine.com/

Published in the United States of America by Medusa Publishing.
Medusa Publishing is a registered trade name of Medusa Publishing, LLC.

First Edition: 2022

Never be afraid to slam that door closed if you're willing to open the next one.

Contents

Episode One Pack 6

Episode Two Fool 11

Episode Three Responsibility 16

Episode Four Chores 22

Episode Five Visit 28

Episode Six Wrong Place 34

Episode Seven Necklace 40

Episode Eight Harvest 50

Episode Nine Run 59

Episode Ten Ash Rock 65

Episode Eleven Cashier and a Prayer 71

Episode Twelve Rogue 77

Episode Thirteen Colorado 83

Episode Fourteen Pack Issues 89

Episode Fifteen New Beginnings 94

Episode Sixteen Not Looking 100

Episode Seventeen Proof 106

Episode Eighteen Breaking Out 112

Episode Nineteen First 118

Episode Twenty Move It, Move It 124

Episode Twenty-One And Go 130

Episode Twenty-Two Tourney 136

Episode Twenty-Three Just Throw It 142

Episode Twenty-Four Winner, Winner 148

Episode Twenty-Five Threw It 155

Episode Twenty-Six Investigation 161

Episode Twenty-Seven Luck of the Irish 166

Episode Twenty-Eight Party 172

Also by *Marcelle Valentine* 179
Teaser 181
Acknowledgments 183
Newsletter 185
About the Author.. 187

Episode One: Pack

Shay

STANDING WITH MY head tilted back, the feel of the sun's rays against my skin is one of the rare joys I have. At this early hour, when the air is still cool enough to cause a slight shiver to pass through me as the breeze dances over the sheen of sweat covering my body, I can be me. This is my favorite time of the day because it is the only time I can release my wolf and just run without facing the ridicule of the other pack members.

I should be grateful that I was taken in at a young age by Alpha Tobias and Luna Adela, even though, rest assured, it was not done out of the kindness of their hearts nor any perceived obligation for one of their pack members. After all, my father directly disobeyed his Alpha when he refused to take the life of a young woman. Rumor has it the woman was the Alpha's true mate, but he rejected her because he deemed her unworthy for the role of Luna. Yet this didn't stop him from sleeping with her, which apparently resulted in an unwanted pregnancy. When Adela discovered the tryst, she demanded that Tobias kill Fay and her unborn child. She was unwilling to allow anyone to remain in the pack who may have the right to challenge her future pups for the position to lead us one day. Even though Tobias rejected Fay he didn't have the heart to kill her, so he passed the task on to his second. My dad, who was Tobias's Beta, received this assignment, but he couldn't complete the deed when he found a very pregnant Fay trying to escape. When she realized what his sudden appearance meant, she dropped to her knees to beg my dad for mercy, pleading for the life of her unborn pup. Instead of following his Alpha's orders he ignored them, helping Fay flee Adela's wrath and the pack lands.

After my dad's blatant disregard of Tobias's command, he was left with only two options: challenge Tobias for the right to be Alpha or be expelled from the pack. He knew leaving meant one thing: we would have to become rogue. This situation rarely ends well for one of our kind. Without the backing of your pack, you become an easy target ripe for the pickings, and any wolf trying to make a name for himself will attack you; not to mention, they forbid you from staying on pack land.

So my dad did what he thought was best, figuring if he won we would all be safe with him as the new Alpha, or if the worst should come to pass and he lost to Tobias, he thought my mom and me would be granted permission to remain in the pack. I was four years old when my dad issued the challenge. Three days later, on my fifth birthday, I lost my dad when he entered the circle; worse, Tobias was not the leader my dad believed him to be. The second he fell, my mom was struck down for being the mate of a traitor. As much as I would like to think my mom wanted to stay with me, I know her true desire was to follow my dad. I had overheard them the night before as my mom begged him to reconsider. She wanted my dad to leave because at least they would be together, declaring a life as a rogue with him was far better than a life without him. The only memory I have of her now is her quiet tear-filled confession that she couldn't face life without him and the look of relief when she knew she would be following my dad to meet the moon goddess.

As Tobias prepared to end my life, Adela interceded on my behalf. Not because I was a child, not because she felt sorry for me, not because I was innocent. No, none of these played any part in her decision. She allowed me to live because she saw in me a cook, a maid, a built-in pup-sitter for the pack, and a whipping post when she needed something to take her frustrations out on. I guess I shouldn't complain; they were well within their rights to kill me or cast me out of the pack when my father refused to follow their orders, so I have done what he couldn't; I do as they command. I remain a loyal pack member suffering all of their abuses because the truth is I am afraid of what will happen if I leave. We are told from a young age what life as a rogue is like, of the brutality you live with daily. I have no place else to go, no family, no friends; thus, I remain in the pack that despises me.

As is expected, the Luna gave the Alpha a pup, a son he could pass the pack to. Since Brady has come of age, the ceremony to pass the title of Alpha for the Half Crest Moon Pack will happen soon. Brady, like his father, is not a kind man. I think it would serve not only him but our pack if he grew up some more before he takes the reins, maybe learn some compassion. There is no reason to treat anyone any lesser than the other members, each of us has our worth, but this is exactly how Tobias does things and how I see Brady continuing. I am Omega. Which puts me at the bottom of the pack hierarchy; I am one step away from being rogue. Taunting and teasing of any member classified as Omega is not discouraged; quite the opposite, the Alpha and Luna support it. They often laugh the hardest when a member slams their dirty dinner plate against my chest or dumps it over my head. Tripping me is not out of line and trashing the room I just finished cleaning is just barrels of fun. I only receive a slight reprieve when other pack leaders come to visit. Except when the Alpha from the White Fang Pack shows up, he's just as hateful as Tobias. But then again, why wouldn't he be since they're brothers. It is rare to have two members from the same family as Alpha, but their father is nothing if not ambitious.

Travis and Colton are Brady's best friends, and of the three, I have to admit Travis is the worst. I do everything in my power to avoid riling his ire. I steer clear of him at all costs because to garner his attention is to engage in a deadly game of cat and mouse. He is meaner than a feral rogue, but the way he looks at me when he thinks no one is paying attention makes my skin crawl. Colton isn't terrible when he's not around Travis and Brady. Don't get me wrong, he will never play the part of my knight in shining armor, but when we are alone, he is a different wolf. His tone softens, and he has even helped me carry the tubs filled with dirty dishes back to the kitchen. This is until one of the guys walks in, then he shoves the bin back into my arm screaming at me to hurry up.

There is only one person who has ever been kind to me; Maggie has remained my only friend since we were little. She doesn't have a mean bone in her body. Still, I can't help but

9

notice she has been pulling away from me the older we get. Her dad is a Delta trained to take up the role of Beta should anything happen to Owen, who happily stepped into the role of Beta after my dad died. He never liked how friendly Maggie was with me. He always thought I was beneath them, and I guess I am in pack society standards. It doesn't make the sting of watching her with Natashia and Sadie any easier. Soon she will be expected to find her mate, and I happen to know from past conversations she is secretly hoping it will be Colton.

Since I am expected to prepare breakfast for the entire pack, I know I will have to head back soon. Yet I remain rooted in place, allowing the sun to caress my nude body. This is the only time I can release my wolf and the only time of the day I feel free. When the sun is cresting the sky, the dew is still clinging to the grass and leaves, and the nocturnal animals are climbing back into their dens. This is the only time I allow my wolf any hint of independence. The only time I'm truly free.

Episode Two: Fool

Shay

RUNNING INTO THE kitchen, I am still trying to straighten my clothes after haphazardly throwing them on in an attempt to get back before anyone noticed.

"Where the heck have you been, Shay? Luna Adela was here looking for you."

"Shit."

"Yeah, and she is not happy. So why are you late?"

"I went for a run."

"You know you have to be here to prepare breakfast, and instead, you went out to let your wolf run wild?"

"Contrary to popular belief, I do still have a wolf, and I need to release her from time to time so she doesn't revolt. Nobody wants a pent-up frustrated, pissed-off she-wolf on their hands. Least of all our illustrious leaders."

"Child, we are Omega. No one here cares about whether we exercise our wolf; however, they will care if their breakfast is not prepared when they are ready to eat. Besides, the longer you suppress your wolf the easier it becomes until one day she will no longer claw at you to get out." I know Nan is right about the breakfast part; the pack does not care if my wolf ever sees the light of day or feels the wind flowing through her fur. Let me make this perfectly clear, I do. I have no desire to lose my wolf, nor do I want to stifle her for so long that she no longer has the strength to come out. I can't fathom any shifter wishing to do this. Why in the name of the moon goddess would you ever want to lose this piece of yourself?

Deciding scrambled eggs, bacon, sausage, and pancakes will be the fastest items I can prepare, I grab the pans to get started. I know I have to hurry if I have any hope of making up the time I lost by letting my wolf linger in the meadow longer than I should have.

"We need to prepare the dough for the biscuits if we are going to serve them with breakfast." By we, she means me, and how could I ever forget the damn biscuits? The Luna would shit bricks if her precious freaking biscuits were not prepared.

Fifteen minutes later, I wipe the sweat from my brow as I toss the last tray in the oven before I turn my attention to making the rest of the food. I love Nan; I just wish our head cook would actually help with the cooking part of the kitchen duties. Most of the time, her assistance usually begins and ends with getting the plates and utensils out for the pack.

"Where the hell have you been?" Adela's sudden arrival startles me enough to make me jump. As a result, I burn myself when I spill the coffee I am transferring into the thermal coffee warmer.

"Shi—" Adela's piercing glare has the word dying on my lips. She thinks females in our pack should not curse unless, of course, the female happens to be her. "Apologies, Luna, I overslept."

"Well, isn't it wonderful you could get some extra sleep while the pack goes hungry," she snarls, and I have to forcibly remind myself not to roll my eyes since no one is starving; breakfast will only be a few minutes late. Adela wrinkles her nose while crossing her arms over her chest, almost daring me to argue. I make the wise choice to hold my tongue.

"Breakfast is nearly ready, ma'am," Nan's response comes out in a flurry as she tries to end the stand-off.

"Are you well-rested, Shay?"

"Yes, ma'am."

"Fantastic, you can begin your day by stripping all the bedclothes before moving on to the curtains. Once you finish those tasks, you can scrub all the floors by hand, and I believe your Alpha would like to have a rack of lamb for dinner. Try not to overcook it this time." She turns to leave before she spins back around to face me. "Oh, by the way, Shay, see that you go to bed early enough to get your ass up to pull your weight for this pack."

I drop my chin averting my eyes. No sense in pissing her off any further. This story seems all too familiar. The only things missing are the fireplace to sleep by, the cartoon mice to assist me in my task, and that damn fairy godmother to grant me some long overdue wishes. She can keep the stupid glass slippers; my wolf has no use for them.

"You really know how to piss off my mom, don't you?" When I turn, I discover Brady tossing a piece of bacon into his mouth.

"It would seem so."

"I am beginning to think it's a talent of yours."

"One I would just as soon give back." I let my eyes linger on Brady for a beat too long, and he does not miss it.

Stepping back he lifts his arms, a sly smile spreading over his face, "Like what you see?"

"I was only.... I was just." Well, that's a pointed question. Shit, why in the hell does this asshole have to be handsome? His appearance is every bit the Alpha he will some day be. He has blonde hair, hazel eyes, and an athletic physique. His daily training is evident by the hard lines of his tone muscles visible through his tight shirt. I know I shouldn't fantasize about him. He is expected to find his mate and mark her, making the girl his in the truest sense of the word before they rise to Alpha and Luna. An Omega is not worthy of such an honor; besides, the only time he deems me worthwhile to speak to is when no one is around.

Raising his eyebrows, he ambles closer, the mischievous grin growing larger with each step as he realizes how much his presence affects me. I try to move away. With any luck, I can keep some space between us. Unfortunately, while my brain is occupied with thoughts of the wolf in here with me, he advances much too fast for me to move and by the time I try, it's already too late as I bump into the stove.

He brushes some of the flour I'm certain is covering my face away. "I asked you a question, Shay. Do you like what you see?" His face is dangerously close to mine; my eyes betray me when they slide down to his mouth. Even though he is a complete egotistical asshole, I have had a secret crush on this man for longer than I can recount, or maybe it isn't as secret as I thought. He pins me between his arms, his body reducing the space between us. Tilting his head to the side so he has a better view, his eyes trail down my body.

"Brady," Travis throws the kitchen door open. I try to move away, but there is no place to go. Travis's evil sneer and wicked eyes delight at having discovered us in this semi-compromising position.

"I was going to say your father is looking for you. He said he needs a hand with something, but I see you already have your hands full with the help."

"I have no idea what you're talking about, buddy. I'm just getting a biscuit hot from the oven," he replies as he reaches around me to grab one before he whispers, "Yeah, I'll take your silence as a solid yes." Straightening up, he laughs, "Go ahead, get your fill."

Embarrassed, I drop my eyes. I cannot believe I thought Brady could actually like me. How could I be such a stupid fool?

"Done already?" Leaning forward, he buries his face into my hair. "Shame. I thought you would have more backbone than that." He pulls back so I can see his eyes. "Pity."

He flips the biscuit in the air before he turns to leave. "Let's go see what the old dog wants."

Travis lingers in the kitchen after Brady leaves. His eyes focus on me for much longer than I like when in reality it was probably only mere seconds before they drop to my breast. Instinctually, I lift my arms to cover them, feeling exposed even though I am fully dressed. When he moves towards me, I back away, my wolf screaming at me not to risk him getting any closer.

The laugh he gives me holds no amusement; on the contrary, it is filled with contempt. He grabs a handful of grapes; a low growl rumbles deep in his chest as he tosses one in his mouth before he turns to leave me alone with my racing heart. Note to self: stay the fuck away from Brady, and while we're at it, most definitely keep the hell away from Travis.

Episode Three: Responsibility

Brady

TEASING SHAY HAS become a favorite pastime of mine. I am well aware she likes me; she has for quite some time now. I admit she is pretty, and while my father could give a shit less if I have my fun with her, he would not be pleased if I put a pup in her. My father has repeatedly told me as much. After all, I am the future Alpha of this pack, where she is one step above the wolves I hunt down and kill for sport.

This is part of the reason I keep my interactions with her PG, yet I can't help flirting with her. I admit the slight blush which crawls across her face every time I do is something I enjoy watching.

Shortly after I turned sixteen, I developed a reputation for being a ladies' man; I have no idea how it started, but I also do nothing to dispel it. Hence the reason I acted like an arrogant asshole in there with Shay. At twenty-two, I should know better; in reality, I do. I hate behaving like this. Hate being a dick, but for some unknown damn reason, my dad thinks higher of me for acting like a pompous, self-serving jerk while I just feel like the ass I am. Thinking about her reactions to my comments, I damn near want to smack the shit out of myself.

Shay is a sweet girl who has no reason to be; the entire pack has not been kind to her. Well, besides Maggie. At least Maggie has treated her with respect. Although lately, Maggie has been spending more time with Natashia, the biggest bitch in the pack. Shay is not the only one on the receiving end of her tirades; every unattached female in this pack faces it at some point. I do not know why any of them put up with her shit. Somehow this crazy girl has convinced herself I will choose her as my Luna. I would sooner chew my own arm off than to be mated to her. Now someone like Shay would make a good leader. To be honest, I came closer to kissing her in there today than I ever have before. I don't know if I would have crossed this line or not. I guess this will have to remain one of life's little mysteries, thanks to my asshat buddy Travis. Speaking of the asshat....

I turn to see if he has followed me out of the kitchen. When I find I am alone in the hall, a pang of frustration rips through me when I realize Travis is still in there with her. I have no idea why the thought of them alone in there bothers me; it just does. I contemplate storming back into the kitchen to pull his ass out when he strides through the door. Looking entirely too pleased with himself.

"What the hell took you so long?"

"Testing the waters."

"I didn't know you were into Shay." The harsh quality of my tone betrays the indifferent attitude I want to present.

"Why? Did you want to keep that tasty piece all for yourself?"

"Nah, I could give a shit less what Shay does or who she screws around with." Hoping to cover my irritation, I slug him in the chest before continuing with a grin, "Even an asshole like you." In some ways, this is true, yet I admit I enjoy being the one who holds her eye.

His smirk pisses me off even as I turn to enter my father's office.

"What took you so long?"

"He was occupied in the kitchen with the…. Help."

"You can leave," I snap.

"I've told you about that girl."

"So you have." My father has an innate way of going for one's throat. He barks his orders and expects everyone to fall in line. Sadly for the old man, I am not like everyone else. Rarely do I comply with most of the things he believes I should, but I would be lying if I didn't admit to still falling in line with other things. My dad thinks I need to further prove my mantle, while my mom thinks the moon rises and sets on me. As the future Alpha, a role I am not even sure I want, I need to prove I am worthy of the position while not being a completely disrespectful ass to him. He still runs this pack, so I will continue carefully weighing my words around him.

"We are hosting the Autumn Harvest ball. Every pack within a hundred miles will attend. Do you understand the importance of this and why we are hosting?" When I do not reply to his question, he proceeds with his lecture, but not before he gives me his patented you better fall in line scowl. "You are expected to have a mate when you take over. So you need to Stop playing with the Damn Help! Do I make myself clear on this?"

"Shay is still a member of this—"

"If you are suggesting she is a member of this pack, you better rethink your statement, son."

"Well, isn't she? What heinous act could this one girl have possibly done to this pack to be treated like we treat her?"

A low growl from my dad informs me I am treading on dangerous ground. "We are done talking about that girl. Pull your head out of your ass. It would behoove you to remember I do not have to choose you to succeed me. Now I suggest you focus on the task at hand."

"I am well aware of why we host this party every year. Let me remind you, I never asked you to make me Alpha, so if you want to give the position to one of your bootlickers...." this grabs his attention along with several others in the room since the snarls are now coming from all sides of me. ".... then go right ahead and name one of them, but it would serve you well to remember having a party does not mean I will find my mate. So, dad, what happens when all your planning goes up in flames if I don't?"

My dad storms around his desk, grabbing my shirt in his fist. His eyes narrow to little more than slits, and his upper lip is twisted in a snarl which is fitting since he barks his response through gritted teeth, "Then you will give up any notion of finding your mate and take one of the she-wolves from this pack or your uncle's. But let me make myself perfectly clear that girl, who is barely a wolf, is not an option."

What the hell? Where is this coming from all of a sudden? What makes him think I would choose Shay? I have never led anyone to believe this. Frustrated, I leap to my feet, inadvertently knocking the chair over in the process. My eyes move from my father to his Beta before glaring at my dumb-ass best friend.

"The thought never crossed my fucking mind, dad."

"Keep it that way. You better god damn remember who her father is, a traitor who tried to reach too high. A worthless traitorous bastard I cut down, and I will not allow his bloodline—"

"I said I have no intention of choosing her."

"Yeah, he just wants to fuck her. Isn't that right, brother?" Travis is pushing his luck with me. This conversation just took a hard right turn, and nothing I say will help at this point. Running my hand through my hair while I take several deep breaths, I decided my best course of action with regard to this topic was to just concede. I guess the only way to prove my loyalty to my pack is to steer clear of Shay. Without another word I throw the door open, stalking out.

"Wait up, Brady." I don't have to turn around to know it's Colton running after me.

"What?"

"Easy man. Damn, are you alright?"

"Just fucking peachy," I snap. I know my frustration is currently being heaped on the wrong man; as a result, I clarify, "Argument with my dad."

"Gotcha."

"Did you need something, Colt?"

"Nah, I was just wondering where you were heading?"

"Out for a run." I have to work off some of the pent-up frustration coursing through me. It is making my wolf anxious. Since Travis interrupted me while I was contemplating a workout of another kind, not to mention the asshole I call dad and his constant overbearing demands on me, I need to release my wolf. I fucking need this run.

"Good, I could use the exercise."

"Try to keep up," I reply as I yank my shirt off before dropping into my wolf's form as we streak into the woods.

Need more time to figure this one out.

Episode Four: Chores

Shay

I KEEP MY head down the rest of the day while trying to complete the ever-growing list of tasks Adela keeps dumping on me. Whenever I think I am close to finishing, she finds me to give me something else that I positively must complete today. Why the hell I need to replant the flowers I just planted two days ago is beyond me, but who am I to argue other than the damn idiot doing these stupid tasks.

Keepyourmouthshut-keep your mouth shut-Keep. Your. Mouth. Shut. This has become my unofficial new mantra. Every muscle in my body is beginning to ache; sitting back on my heels, I swipe my hand across my brow. The sound of shrill laughter sends a ripple of irritation coursing through me when I realize who will soon invade my space. I don't have to see their faces to know who is coming through the door....

"He will not be able to take his eyes off you," the ass-kisser declares.

Natashia and Sadie! Of course, it would have to be these two. Oh, and by the way, for easy reference, Natashia is the bitch, and Sadie is the ass-kisser, and neither of them believes I am anything more than trash to be cast aside. This works for me since I don't rank them too high on the evolutionary pyramid either. What irritates me the most about them is they both seem to have an innate sixth sense to know when I am busy cleaning the messes they and the rest of the elite pack members made because they appear every time I am down on my hands and knees scrubbing floors or toilets.

To make matters worse, they are both dressed to impress in amazing clothes without a speck of dirt or a wrinkle anywhere on them, while I look like I just pulled mine out of the dirty clothes hamper. The saddest part is seeing Maggie, the only friend I have ever had, with them. I am aware she has been socializing more and more with these two. Even though I know she only does it hoping to spend more time with Colton, it doesn't change the fact that seeing her with them stings just a little bit. Especially because I know she is aware of how bad these two make my life.

Since they are so preoccupied regaling Natashia's outfit, I pray they will take no notice of me over here trying to scrape gum off the bottom of the table. Who does this shit? I mean, hello, the trash can is literally fifteen feet from the damn table. Seeing as my current task involves me crammed under a table, I have a fairly good chance of staying off their radar, at least until I finish this utterly embarrassing chore.

"Ophelia!" And there goes any hope of these three just passing through. Ophelia is not like the other girls in the pack. She's a few years older than us, and while I would not call her a friend, she is not blatantly cruel to me either. She tends to keep her opinions to herself unless she is with her best friend Rose, in which case she has no shortage of things to say. Most of which center around Natashia and Sadie. I think it's comical how she describes Natashia as a shallow little girl. Truth be told, I find the entire situation humorous since every time Natashia sees Ophelia, she tries to pretend like they are the best of friends. How do I know what Ophelia actually thinks of them? It's really pretty simple. The only element you need to discover people's most intimate thoughts is to be invisible. Since the only time anyone around here seems to notice me is when they are barking orders at me, I'm about as invisible as you can get. Well, except for Natashia and Sadie, they make it their life's mission to make mine a living hell.

"Oh, hey Tosh." A nickname Natashia insists her friends call her, which is just another way for her to show what category she has put you into. You either fall into the important people category, the everyone else lineup, or in my case, the nobody class. "What are you up to today?"

"Dress shopping for the big shindig," she says with one of her holier-than-thou smiles plastered across her face.

"I assume you found one based on your beaming smile."

"Goddess, yes, and it's amazing! Isn't it, Sadie?"

"Yeah, I loved it the second I saw it. I thought about getting it, but then Tosh saw it…. And well, you know."

"Oh, stop whining will you! It looks better on me anyway." I can see the smile on Sadie's face falter. I have no idea why any sane person would subject themself to the kind of abuse Natashia doles out like Pestilence does with the plague. Yeah, I totally just compared the bitch with one of the horsemen of the apocalypse. What of it?

Returning my attention to the current task, I try my best to remain quiet. I have zero desire to draw their attention over toward my direction. My plan works out just fine until the putty knife I'm using slips and cuts into the hand I was bracing myself with.

"Owwww," the word is out of my mouth before I have time to think about the consequences.

"Well—well—well, if it isn't Red." Yeah, 'cause that joke never gets old. The nickname red is actually a reference to Little Red Riding Hood. In the original version, the dumb little girl ends up being eaten by the big bad wolf. Apparently, these morons have never read any of the later versions. You know the ones where a woodcutter or huntsman busts into the cabin where the wolf is sleeping after filling his belly full of grandmother and Red, only to cut him open, releasing both grandma and Red before they fill his stomach with rocks. When the wolf goes outside to drink from the well, he falls down inside it because of the weight of the stones and ends up drowning. Yeah, this is a great analogy to tell around a bunch of wolf shifters. Besides, the biggest problem with their stupid insult is: One, I'm a wolf also, and two, I don't need anyone to rescue me. I learned early on I only have myself to rely on.

Perhaps if this girl spent more time studying in high school rather than opening her legs for all the male teachers to get her grades, she might have a higher intellect. Although I found it hilarious when one of the male teachers never got around to fixing her grades after she blew him and ended up missing the entire last half of the school year when he broke his pelvis. The scuttlebutt was one of our male student teachers planned on taking over his class until he could return to work. Natashia couldn't wait since she was always sniffing around the poor guy like a dog in heat, which I guess she kind of is. Imagine her surprise when the district brought in a more permanent female teacher to whom she couldn't manipulate or offer sexual favors. Needless to say, she failed English Lit her senior year and had to take summer classes to get her diploma. Best weeks of my life.

"What are you doing over there?"

"Work. Something I'm certain a princess like yourself would know nothing about," I mutter.

"What was that? You need to take the shit out of your mouth," she says before laughing like a crazy-ass loon.

"Cleaning."

"What could you possibly be cleaning, hiding under a table?"

I decide not to respond to her. It's best just to let this one slide. Hopefully, her desire to talk to Ophelia will outweigh her desire to make my day any worse.

"She is scraping gum from the tables," Sadie yells. Which makes two of the four girls laugh so hard they may actually piss their pants. I don't miss the sad smile Maggie gives me before averting her eyes down to the floor. Either she doesn't like them laughing at me, she is afraid I may call her out for not stepping in to end their cackling, or her shoes just became the most fascinating object in the entire room. No worries, Maggie, I would never expect you to stand up to them for me.

"Well, isn't that just the saddest damn thing you've ever heard of? I always wondered who got stuck with that job. I guess now we know." Natashia's gloating attitude is only making this entire interaction worse.

I realize she has no intentions of leaving me alone to finish this shit job, so I decide to extricate myself from the situation.

Fingers crossed, she keeps her happy ass right here while I move on to the next task at hand.

"Did you get your cape for the big day, Red? Oh, what am I talking about? This is by invitation only, and no one in their right mind would want to invite you. Isn't that right, little Cinder girl?"

Oh, for the love of Pete, this chick really needs to come up with some better insults. Listen, I may compare my life to a certain princess made famous by Disney; this does not mean I am okay with the bitch doing it.

"My cape and basket are both ready and waiting. Thanks for asking." I push through the door to the kitchen as I finish, "Here's hoping you don't end up with a belly full of rocks by the end of the event."

"What did you say?" She hisses. Thankfully, the door swings shut before I can respond.

"You really need to quit riling her up before we all get in trouble."

"Don't worry, Nan. The only one around here who has to fret about getting in trouble with the Luna is yours truly."

Episode Five: Visit

Brady

*A*S MUCH AS I would like to say, releasing my wolf is enough to quiet the echoes of rage my father is such a fucking pro at eliciting from me; unfortunately, I can't. Hell, not only did I run across our lands, I ended up all the way over within my uncle's territory. And after I crossed his borders, I continued running even as Colton yelled for me to stop.

When one of his scouts spotted me, I didn't have enough time to shift back before they took off to warn the pack of my intrusion. Ordinarily, when you plan to cross onto another pack's lands, it is customary to let them know you are coming; this way, they expect you. What I just did was invade their territory, and while I have an open invitation from my uncle, the scout did not recognize my wolf. As soon as the scout took off, I shifted back to my human form to wait for the sentries I know will be here soon. No point in making this matter any worse than I already have. This is why I am currently leaning against a damn rock, waiting to see who will get here first, the sentries or Colt.

"Damn Brady, you were running like the devil was after you," Colton tells me as he shifts back into his human form before he collapses, panting hard.

"Hey, I tried to tell you," I laugh as I toss some loose stones lying next to me at him.

"I might need a minute before we head back. Damn, I didn't realize you planned on crossing two counties."

"Don't worry about it; take all the time you need. We have to stay until—" the low growls of several approaching wolves cut my response short. Colton scrambles to his feet as he backs closer to where I am leaning against the rock. As I continue tossing the stones in my hand at a can I spotted across the way, my calm demeanor doesn't seem to put him, or our new arrivals, at ease.

The two who are currently stalking the clearing I don't recognize. One moves right as the other goes left. Their backs hunch up, their tales pulled tight, and their heads are low as they approach. They want me to know they do not appreciate a wolf from another pack on their lands; they will have no issues defending it, even if it means their death. Based on the size of the wolves circling us, I would have to say they sent a couple of their elite to investigate who we are. The closer they get without shifting back, I realize these two may be more of the attack first, ask questions later kind of soldiers.

Just when I believe I may need to shift back to teach these two a lesson, a third wolf enters the clearing, and this one I recognize right away; it's Zeb, my uncle's Beta. While I imagine he will read me the riot act for not following the proper protocol, I know I will no longer have to fight anyone from within my uncle's pack. My dad would have my damn head for something like that.

"Brady, what the hell are you doing here? Is everything okay with your pack?"

"Yeah."

"So, want to tell me what the hell you're doing here without telling us you were coming?"

"I went out for a run."

"A run?"

"A long run?" My questioning response has him shaking his head as a slight chuckle escapes him. "Matt, Link, this is our Alpha's nephew, Brady. Brady, this is Matt—"

"And Link. Yeah, I caught that. Sorry to make you guys come out here to investigate." Both men shift back to their human forms. I have to admit I'm damn glad I didn't have to fight these two because Link is the size of a fucking tank.

"Zeb, you think we could grab some grub before heading home?"

"I know I'm starving," Colt interjects.

"Would you like anything else, princess," Zeb snaps, but I hear the amusement in his response.

"A warm bath and foot rub wouldn't hurt."

"You ever gonna grow up, kid?" I laugh as I drop into my wolf to follow them back to their packhouse. Thankfully, Matt offers both Colt and me something to wear when we arrive. While most shifters don't care who sees us without clothes, it is probably best to cover up during dinner. Uncle Sebastian pulls me in for a hug when he sees me, clapping me on the back several times.

"Didn't know you were coming."

"It's kind of an impromptu visit." His eyebrow furrows as he tilts his head. Since I am not in the mood to rehash the shit between dad and me with my uncle, I decide not to elaborate any further. He'll find out when he talks to dad. Tonight I just want to have a good time. This thought materializes no sooner than I notice a girl leaning against a table staring at me. If the smile alone isn't enough to tell me she's interested, the fact that she hasn't taken her eyes off me even though she seems to be in the middle of a conversation with the other girls at the table certainly does.

Taking my seat at my uncle's table, I focus on the conversation around me, yet I can feel her eyes still directed at me. She is definitely not my mate; if she were, I would have realized it the second I saw her, but that doesn't mean I don't find her sexy as hell. Glancing in her direction, I don't miss the long, lean legs she has out on display, not to mention the low-cut shirt she has on is doing nothing to cover her cleavage. Her breast, while not as big as Shay's.... What the hell? Why am I thinking of Shay right now? After running for three hours, I managed to get this girl out of my head, only to have her creep right back in the first time I see a set of fine-looking tits. Maybe everybody is right; I should just fuck her and get it over with. Once her allure is gone, I may stand a chance of getting my damn head on straight.

The blonde who started this whole internal monolog smiles at me again before running her fingers sensually down her neck. She doesn't miss my eyes tracking her hand. Shaking my head, I give her a half-grin before turning to talk to my cousin.

"Hey, Jason, who's that girl over there?"

"You mean the blonde who's been giving you the come fuck me eyes the entire night?"

"Ah, I guess."

"Nah, if you can't be more assertive than that, then you definitely can't handle Erin."

"Shut up, dumbass. So what's her story? Is she mated to anyone?"

"If she was, do you think she would be eye-banging you with the hopes of riding your coc–" the glare I give him cuts the word off before he can finish. I mean what the hell, my aunt, his mom, is sitting two chairs away from us, for Christ's sake.

"Oh, I'm sorry. Have I offended your delicate sensibilities?"

"No, I just have more sense than you, apparently."

"She ain't attached to anyone, although she's looking." I watch as she licks her lips before pulling the bottom one into her mouth.

"I swear, is there a damn class these girls all take on the art of fucking seduction, or are men really this weak when it comes to the opposite sex?"

"We're just this weak," Colt replies as he watches blondie get up and head in our direction. "Why the hell can't girls like her want a nice guy like me?"

"Because not only do you scream Delta but just looking at you, I can see she would chew you up and spit you out," my cousin tells him.

"Did you ever date her?"

"Does it matter, cuz?"

"Yeah, it kinda does matter to me."

"Then no, I never dated her. Have fun," Jason says just as the girl arrives at our table.

"Hi, my name's—" The first thing I notice is the slight twang of a southern accent.

"Erin, yeah, I know."

"You noticed me?"

"You've had your eyes glued to him the entire night, Darlin; the entire pack noticed you," Jason interrupts. Her cheeks flare red from his comment. He didn't have to be such an asshole about it.

I decide to make it up to her by saying, "You're kind of hard to miss."

"Awww, that's so sweet of you to say. See Jason, you don't have to be a complete jerk all the time."

"Whatever you say, sugar."

Shaking my head, I stand before asking, "Would you like to take a walk with me?"

Episode Six: Wrong Place

Shay

*A*FTER FINISHING THE last of the chores Adela so generously heaped on me, I decide to take advantage of the pleasant evening before winter makes an appearance and steals these nights away from me. Thanks to my wolf, while the cold does not affect me like it would a non-shifter, it doesn't mean I enjoy sitting outside knee-deep in snow. Our pack lands are located in the northern portion of Montana, and we tend to get a fair amount of snow.

Sitting on the swing, I rest my head against the chain while letting the day's events slip away. All except one, my interaction in the kitchen with Brady. I really can't explain why I am so drawn to him. I know he is not my mate; from what everyone describes, the connection to your mate is all-consuming, and while I may have fantasized about him on more than one occasion, I don't get that all-consuming vibe. Besides, it's not like Brady is knocking on my bedroom door at night to keep me company. Do I want him to knock on my door? Now there's the million-dollar question.

"Were you hoping to find me out here?" Travis asks, leaning in next to my ear. Hell, I was so lost in my thoughts of a certain soon-to-be Alpha that I didn't hear him walk up behind me. This goes against every one of my instincts, not to mention my number one rule, which is to steer clear of Travis at all cost.

When I try to stand, he stops me by wrapping one of his arms around my chest; I don't miss where his arm is resting across my breast, further confirming every last one of my concerns about him.

"Whoa, no need to take off so quick, Shay."

"I have to finish the list Luna Adela gave me."

"If you still had work to do, what are you doing out here, and what put that," he reaches around, placing his finger to my mouth, "smile on your face?"

My heart ramps up and pounds against my chest from the unwanted contact. Travis is way too close for comfort. I guess his mom never taught him the concept of not invading another individual's personal space. When he leans over further to bring his mouth closer to mine, I know I need to put some distance between us before he takes this any further.

"So, are you going to tell me what you're doing out here? If not, I'm sure we can think of something else to do." His arm, which is still resting across my breast, shifts. My initial thought was maybe he would let go of me, but when he did it two more times, I realized this asshole was feeling me up. I know this is about to go from bad to worse. My only hope is I can remove myself before it shifts to that worse situation plaguing my mind, so I have to be careful as I weigh my words.

"I had to wait until Nan finished in there before I could wrap up cleaning the kitchen. She must be done by now, so I should get back to work." I shift enough to give me enough room to slip off the swing and out of his grasp in one quick move. Not wanting to have my back to this asshole, I turn to look at him while I go back towards the packhouse. His eyes are glued to mine, and the malicious intent I discover in them is alarming.

You need to get away from him right now, Shay. My wolf growls in my head.

I know, but if I run, we will just make this a deadly game where we become the prey. I try to reason with my wolf.

He's dangerous. I don't like the way he looks at us.

Just stay calm. We'll be in the packhouse in another second.

What if no one is around? What will you do then, Shay?

I'll figure it out. Just please stop growling at me.

Realizing exactly how close I am to safety, or as close to safety as someone in my position can be, I chance turning my back while I pick up my pace. Just before I can run up the stairs, Travis is on me. He leans in, effectively pinning me between the railing and his body.

"Did I ever tell you how much I love your blonde hair?"

"No," I say, and getting that one word out took effort.

"I do, but it makes me wonder." I don't care what he is wondering about. I just want to be anywhere other than here. His body presses against mine as he brings his mouth to my ear. "Do you want to know what I wonder about?"

"I really need—"

"The kitchen can wait, Shay." I always wear my hair pulled up in a ponytail. I do this to keep my long locks out of my way while cooking and cleaning. He pulls my hair out of the band, allowing it to fall around my shoulders. Picking up a section of my unruly mane, he twirls it between his fingers. He does this for several seconds. When he finally drops it, I see an opportunity to dip under his arm, a path for my escape, but he has his hand on my hip before I can.

"I wonder if I would discover the same color…. In other places too."

Jerking my head to look at him fully, I snap, "Get the fuck off of me."

"I'll take that as a yes. Now I want to see it for myself even more than I did before. What do you say, Shay? Do you want to show me?" I push past him only to have him snatch out to grab my arm, yanking me back into his chest. "You think Brady wants you, a little nobody who is barely considered a member of this pack? He's fucking playing with you."

"Is that why you want this nobody so damn much?" I snarl. His icy glare turns deadly as his wolf struggles to break free. Even his wolf is an asshole, but what did I expect of him? After all, he had to live within this braindead dick his entire existence. Thankfully before he can respond, headlights splash across us, lighting up our surroundings. His vicious glare stays on me until the car pulls in front of the packhouse. As he turns to see who just arrived, his grip remains painfully tight around my arm. I have little doubt tomorrow I will find a hand-shaped bruise there.

He does not release me until he sees Brady and Colton climbing out of the car. He may not be my knight in shining armor, but hell, I'll take whatever I can get right now because the alternative is lashing out at this sadistic asshole and risk being banished by the Alpha and Luna.

"This isn't over yet, Shay," Travis's quiet hissed response has his desired effect when chills race down my spine and put my body on high alert. He shoves me hard into the railing to further drive home his point. The impact knocks the wind out of me and leaves me gasping for my next breath as he turns to saunter towards the car.

I turn my head just in time to see Brady lean over and kiss the girl who drove them home. I don't remember ever seeing this girl around here, and as painful as this is to admit, the girl is stunning. She has beautiful blonde hair, and yes, I know I technically have blonde hair, but mine does not glisten as hers does. I hear Travis laughing when Brady walks toward him.

"Damn brother, who the hell was that hot piece of ass?"

"Her name is Erin; she is a member of my uncle's pack."

"If all his female pack members look like her, I may need to switch packs," he says before he leans down slightly so he can wave at the girl backing out.

"You think my uncle would want your sorry ass in his pack?" Brady laughs, slugging him before throwing his arm around his shoulder to lead him back into the packhouse. Pushing further into the shadows, I wish I could just disappear. I have no desire to come face to face with Brady after what just happened between his best friend and me.

I try to slink around the corner of the porch before they get any closer, but like a few minutes ago, Travis ends any hopes of escape.

"What are you doing over there, Shay?"

"Shay?" Brady questions as he looks around Colt. For one brief second, I contemplate snapping and telling Travis he knows damn good and well what I am doing over here since he was the one who held me here against my will.

"Damn, Brady, you must have a golden dick. You got them lining up as they all wait on your ass to come home."

"You asshole," I yell.

"Whoa, cool your jets, sweetheart; there is plenty of him to go around." I don't know why I thought Brady would put an end to his taunts because he doesn't. Reminding me once again I am really and truly alone in this world. Looking from Brady, who has a questioning look covering his face, over to Travis whose grin holds no amusement, I do the only thing I can think of; I turn and bolt for the woods.

Episode Seven: Necklace

Shay

THE NIGHT I ran into the woods, I considered not stopping. I have never been so close to turning away from the only home I ever knew; instead, I curled into a ball and cried myself to sleep. I am normally stronger than this, a side effect of living without any love for most of my life. I had to toughen my skin, harden my heart, and until tonight I have not cried, not one single tear since a week after my parents died. It was the night Adela told me I had a choice to make. I could either accept my fate and move on or get the hell out of her pack because she would not have someone's sniveling brat ruining her day. Imagine being five years old and having every wolf's fear thrust on you, facing life on your own as a rogue; I learned how to hold my tears at bay real quick. I made it back in the nick of time to cook their breakfast the next morning. Goddess knows I don't need Adela coming down on my ass for the same thing she just chewed me out about.

Five days have passed since that moment of weakness. And since I have not seen hide nor hair of Travis or Brady for that matter, it has been a blissfully uneventful couple of days. This has worked out in my favor since the Autumn Harvest Ball is in two days, and Adela has kept me extremely busy. Glancing at the clock on the wall, I see it is already a quarter to twelve. I have one last thing I need to do before falling into bed. Rushing into the laundry room, I discover more than I bargained for when I find Ophelia and Rose locked in a passionate embrace.

"Shit, I'm so sorry." I fumble to yank the door closed as I hurry away from the door as Rose begs Ophelia to stop me.

"Hey…. Hey! God damn it, I'm talking to you." Ophelia runs up behind me, grabbing my arm. I flinch, not just because the contact is unwanted but also because her grasp is in the exact spot Travis clutched me the night the mysterious blonde brought Brady home. While the bruises have begun to fade, the contact is still unpleasant.

"What the fuck do you think you're doing?"

"I was just coming in to fold the last of the laundry."

Ophelia steps directly up to me, "If you even think about telling anybody what you saw tonight, I will make your life a living hell." Great, just one more person to make my life miserable, but neither Ophelia nor Rose has anything to worry about from me because I have no intention of telling anybody anything. It shouldn't even be an issue, but the pack frowns on it because if Ophelia and Rose stay together, then it reduces the likelihood of them being able to have pups which is all that Tobias cares about. Growing the damn pack. Hell, he turned his own back on his mate because he didn't deem her worthy; there is no way he will understand or care that Ophelia and Rose are in love with each other.

41

"I don't know what you're talking about. I didn't see you tonight."

"I fucking saw you, Shay. And I swear to the moon goddess if you—"

"Ophelia, I said I didn't see you tonight," I say this in a way I hope she understands that while yes, I saw what was happening between her and Rose, I won't say a word about it.

Ophelia's chest is still rising and falling. Obviously, she was prepared for the fight she believed she would have on her hands to halt me tattle-telling on them. On the other hand, Rose has tears shining in her eyes while several others trickle down her cheeks. With me being so low in the pack they probably figured I would try to use this against them to gain favor with whoever the hell would care about something like this, but one, I'm not a complete asshole, and two, who the hell am I to judge anyone for who they wanna bang, who they like or love. Hoping to set their minds at ease, I place my hand on Ophelia's while looking directly at Rose as I repeat, "I saw nothing. I do not know what you're talking about. I wasn't there. I stayed in my room the entire night tonight."

Ophelia visibly relaxes. Her eyes assess my face while she decides if she can trust what I am saying. When she finally arrives at her conclusion, she dips her head at me before cradling Rose protectively in her embrace.

*****

Since discovering them last night, I can't help but notice Ophelia and Rose have made themselves scarce all day. That is until supper when everyone, except for the scouts and sentries on patrol, is expected to be in the dining hall for dinner.

Brady also returned today, along with Travis and Colton. I assume he went to see his mystery girl and took the dickhead and Tweedle Dee with him. Although I have no idea why you would want to take your buddies along while hooking up with your new girlfriend. But hey who am I to notice what our future Alpha does, a nobody who better get the next course out to the illustrious pack if I know what's good for me, that's who.

Carrying a tray full of food out, I see Natashia has graced us with her presence, which is great, just fan-fucking-tastic. I had hoped whatever hole she was wallowing in would swallow her up but nope, here she is looking like the regal bitch princess she always does. I don't miss her icy gaze flicking to mine when I enter the room, nor Adela's, who is listening intently to something Natashia is whispering to her.

Ignoring them both, I return to the task at hand as I deliver the first plate to Tobias, then Brady, followed by Adela's, and as I am setting the final dish in front of the bitch herself, Adela's words bring a halt to me serving anyone else.

"Nan, if you and some of the other Omegas could please finish serving the rest of the pack, I need to have a word with this one." Nan's eyes flick to mine before she dips her head and begins serving the remaining people.

"Where were you last night, Shay?"

"I was here."

"And what were you doing while *you was here?*" her last words mimic my tone.

"Did I do something wrong, Luna?"

"That is what I am trying to ascertain." When I do not say anything further, Adela proceeds.

"It has come to my attention that a valuable necklace has gone missing." Is she asking me if I saw anything? Surely she

43

cannot be accusing me; however, when she pulls her lips into a thin line while Natashia's lips tip up slightly, I realize this is precisely what she is doing.

"You don't think I took it, do you?"

"Natashia advised the necklace—" Of course, it was Natashia who leveled the accusation against me. "was in her room when she left at 11:40, and when she returned ten minutes later, it was gone. The only person she saw in the hall was you as you scampered around the corner."

I can't believe I am being accused of stealing from a member of this pack. I have served them all loyally, albeit I admit to secretly begrudging every second of it. Every second of them looking down at me, not to mention their constant reminders of who my father was. A man I remember as a strong and loving man, yet someone they accused of being a traitor for refusing to kill a pregnant woman. Of course, I cannot openly call Natashia a liar because the only way I can prove my innocence is by admitting to being with Ophelia and Rose when the necklace supposedly went missing. The issue with me bringing them into this is Adela would insist on knowing what we were doing, and I have no legitimate reason for being with them or at least none that I can think of right now. I have never been a good liar; my stupid face gives me away every time I try.

"Where were you last night?!!!" My focus is mainly on the ground, but I do not miss the fleeting look of concern crossing Ophelia's face.

"Is this entirely necessary right now, love? I am trying to eat my supper." Alpha says.

"Theft can never be overlooked, dear husband." Her eyes move over to me, and I can see every ounce of hate and disdain she has for me in her icy stare. "One we must rip out root and stem. Regardless of the time of day."

"It was just a necklace, mom."

"An extremely expensive one, son." When there is no further protest from the men in her life, she drums her fingers on the table as she waits for my response.

"I didn't take it. You can search my room if you want."

"Yeah, cause you'd be dumb enough to hide it there," Natashia snarls.

"Where the hell else would I put it, Natashia?"

"You're always sneaking out of here early in the morning. You could have hidden it just about anywhere."

"Why would I steal your necklace?" What I want to say is I don't need your stupid necklace. I have one, but I don't want any of these people to know about it, so I hold my tongue beyond my initial question.

"Jealousy. Who knows why low-lives like you do what they do." Her response has a low growl rumbling from my wolf. This bitch just took it entirely too far.

"You will control your wolf and answer the question right now, Shay!" Adela demands.

Looking up at the ceiling, I work hard to get my wolf under control. She is furious. As I bring my eyes back down to meet Adela's gaze, they land on Rose's face for a second. The only thing I see staring back at me is terror. Making my decision easy, "I was in my room."

"The entire night."

"Yes, ma'am."

"Can anyone confirm this?"

"No, Luna, I was alone."

"Well, in that case, I will have to assume the information Natashia has provided me is correct, and since both versions cannot be true, it would appear you're lying. As such, you will pay back the injured party in full."

"I don't have that kind of money, Luna."

"Well then, I guess your Alpha and I will have to pay for it since you claim you have no money...." How the hell could I possibly have money? They sure as shit don't pay for being at their beck and call, and since Adela is hell-bent on making my life hell, she leaves me no time to get a job anywhere else. So yeah, I only have a couple hundred dollars to my name hidden away, and I sure as fuck ain't giving that to Natashia. ".... you will owe it to us. We will hold your pay," Pay? What fucking pay? "and cut your rations in half until you have paid back every cent you owe." Well, that is just fuckin grand. It's not like they give me much food as it is. I am acutely aware my next question is poking the bear and will only add to my misery, but I can't help myself.

"And how much do I owe?" I ask the question with more force than I intended, and it does not go unnoticed by anyone in the room.

"Watch your tone. You're in enough trouble.... Unless you have a burning desire to face further punishment."

Keepyourmouthshut—keep your mouth shut. Keep. Your. Mouth. Shut. Shay! I gnash my teeth together, my jaw clenching and relaxing as I try to hold my tongue. Praying my mantra can help with that.

"You owe fifteen hundred dollars."

"Fifteen hundred?" I repeat in stunned disbelief.

"Did I stutter?" Letting out an exasperated sigh, I turn to walk away. "I did not dismiss you. Did anyone hear me say she was dismissed?"

Closing my eyes, I take several deep breaths before facing the woman who has made it her personal life's mission to make mine miserable. If she planned to treat me like shit my entire life, she should have just tossed my ass to the rogues when I was a kid and been done with it. Squaring my shoulders, she might be able to control much of my life, but I will not permit her to take even one more ounce of my self-respect. As a result, I lift my chin slightly higher in defiance of the ruler. Adela keeps me pinned within her icy glare for several more seconds before she snaps, "Get back to work, Shay. You owe us a lot of money, and standing here like a lost pup isn't paying us back."

What I want to say is I tried to go back to work until you called me back so you could stare at me for a couple more seconds, try to continue humiliating me in front of the entire pack, and give the assholes sitting around you something to snicker about. Yet I am smart enough to know if I had said any of these things, I would have found my ass strapped to a post while Travis whipped me mercilessly. I am starting to think living as a rogue may be preferential to this shit, but if everything I've heard about the life of a rogue is true, I may find myself in a worse situation with zero means of escape.

Once their entertainment is over, most pack members return to their homes or rooms here in the packhouse. Of course, they leave their damn plates for me to clean up. Grabbing the tub I use to carry the dirty dishes in, I return to the dining hall only after I am positive the Luna and Alpha are gone, not to mention Brady's gang of assholes.

I manage to clean three tables before I feel a hand on my shoulder. Most of the time, I am hyper-aware of my surroundings, making it damn near impossible for anyone to sneak up on me, but I am so preoccupied with what options I have that I let my defenses drop enough that someone has managed to do just that. Spinning, fully prepared to defend myself if need be, I only relax when I find Ophelia standing there. Aware she may have startled me, she raises her hands to chest level as she takes several steps away from me.

"I just wanted to thank you for not…. You know, telling Tobias and Adela about Rose and me."

Turning back towards the table, I respond, "I told you before; I don't have any idea what you are referring to."

"I know you did, but you have to understand people say things all the time they have no intention of honoring."

"Lucky for you, I'm not most people."

"Yeah, I kind of learned that about you tonight. I want you to know I feel shitty that you have to pay back something I know you didn't take."

"It is what it is."

"Even still, I have a little bit of money—"

"No, I won't take your money. I didn't do what I did so you would owe me something."

"I know that; it's just—"

As I turn my full attention to her, I tell her, "I said no, Ophelia." The last thing I need is to end up owing anyone else. Owing the Luna and Alpha is bad enough.

She raises her hands in an, okay I get it, motion. Wanting to finish up this shit of a day, I move to the next table. My stomach growls loud enough to be heard across the room. Releasing a sigh, I shake my head looking down at the uneaten food on the plate. It must be freaking nice to have so much to eat you can leave over half of it on your plate. Hell, if you take the leftovers on this plate, cut it in half, and then cut it in half two more times, that is what my previous standard portion was, and now it's going to be even less. I will definitely have to resort to hunting small game if I have any hope of surviving as I pay back the ridiculous sum of money.

"At the very least, let me bring you some food."

"Do you think I'm some damn charity case?" I snap. I'm not really mad at Ophelia. She didn't do anything wrong except simply stand here trying to thank me. And to repay her kindness, I act like a fucking whiney child.

I let out another deep breath before I look up but leave my back to Ophelia.

"Thanks, but if they find it, they would just think I stole it, and I can't imagine Adela will be so forgiving if she believes I stole from the pack again after being convicted once."

"I would tell them I gave it to you."

Her earnest response takes me off guard. No one has ever been willing to take responsibility for their actions when I am the one being accused of their crime. This includes Maggie, who allowed me to be whipped on more than one occasion when we were children for something stupid she did. Hell, I still bear the scars from some of those beatings. I also need to keep in mind that nothing comes without a price. Spinning to return to the kitchen, I pause when I arrive next to Ophelia to offer her a piece of sound advice, "You don't want to be associated with me, and more specifically, you don't want them seeing you being nice to me. The leaders of this pack tend not to like it. The best thing you can do for you and Rose, the only way to keep you and your secret safe, is to stay far, far, far away from me."

Episode Eight: Harvest

Brady

"HEY, TRAV," I yell, chasing after him. When we left the dining hall, several of us ended up in my dad's office. My mom continued her tirade about Shay's alleged transgressions and is now demanding my dad whip Shay until she learns her lesson. I began to speak up until Travis interjected. His response to my mom has me completely confused about what could be happening between Shay and him since he just privately offered to pay for the necklace. I don't know if he did it to calm my mom down or if he wants to do it so Shay owes him. Either way, I plan on finding out.

"What's up?"

"Why the hell would you offer to bail Shay out?"

"Didn't you hear man?"

"Hear what?"

"Shay and I are keeping one another warm at night."

Damn, talk about left field. If I am being truthful, I don't have any claims to the girl; I simply didn't realize they were seeing one another. Nor do I understand when they could have had the opportunity because Travis, Colton, and I have been spending extra time at my uncle's pack for the last several weeks. My father and uncle decided our packs should start training with one another. There is some nonsense about how we can learn from them, and they can learn from us. "Since when?"

"Since the night you found that desirable piece of ass from your uncle's pack. What was her name? Oh yeah, Erin, right?"

"Really?"

"Yeah, I was just coming back from a run, and she practically threw herself at me. It started right over there against the rail. She got a little shy when you and Colt showed up, but all those reservations disappeared when she showed up at my door that night."

I don't know what pisses me off more, the fact that they're screwing or that she's the one who started it. Especially since she's always acting like she's terrified of Travis. Maybe she really is full of shit. Perhaps I have been the damn fool around here; it is possible she is everything everyone has claimed. Suddenly I don't feel so fucking bad for her.

Shay

I don't know if I'm more pissed off at Adela, Natashia, or myself. After all, I'm the dumb ass who keeps putting up with this shit. I could just leave; I should just leave. No matter how obedient I am, no matter how much I try to be a part of this pack, the simple fact is I know I never will be.

Tonight is the big event, the Fall Harvest Ball, and I am expected to have everything ready. Thankfully everyone has left me alone to let me get through this never-ending list. First thing this morning, Adela dropped off what I am supposed to wear tonight, and surprise—surprise, it is clearly meant for a server. That's fine by me. I mean, it's not like I thought I would be attending the Ball. A ball I was never permitted to be present at before. I don't know why Adela would think this year would be any different. I can serve them their shit, and when service is done, I can slip back to my room and relax the rest of the night.

"Hi, Shay," I don't have to look up to know who is standing behind me.

"Hi, Maggie."

"So, how have you been?" Now she wants to know how I've been. It's ironic since she has treated me like I'm a damn social leper for weeks. I get that she is only doing it in the hopes of Colt noticing her, but don't expect me to be okay with it.

"What do you want, Maggie?"

"I just wanted to see how you're doing."

"Really? You want to know how I'm doing. Let's see, I am now the sole person responsible for cleaning, cooking, and serving around here. I am expected to watch all the youngest pack members when I am not busy doing everything else. Apparently, I am a thief now, and the only friend I thought I had hasn't talked to me for a month, electing to hang out with the one person who makes it her goal in life to make mine miserable. So yeah, I'm fucking great; how about you, Maggie?" Her face reveals how much the things I just said hurt her, and now I feel like an asshole. This is just me taking my frustration out on the wrong person.

"I'm...."

"Sorry, Maggie, I'm just irritated. I took it out on you, and I shouldn't."

"Why are you talking to this despicable piece of shit?" Natashia's shrill voice is dripping with disdain. I contemplate showing her precisely how despicable I can be but decide better of it. After all, I'm in enough trouble as it is; no point compounding it by knocking this bitch on her ass. I seriously have no damn idea what the hell I did to this chick to elicit the level of hate she heaps on me.

"I was just.... We were...." I can't stand how much Natashia rattles Maggie. I have no idea why she would want to subject herself to this kind of treatment.

"If you want to continue our friendship, I recommend you get one thing straight." Her head whips in my direction, her eyes narrowing to little more than slits before she lifts her nose; the act causes a look of disgust to cross her face as she hisses, "We do not associate with nobodies. You know, like her."

I can't help the eye roll I give her while a disingenuous snort escapes me. Yep, that's me, a nobody. I can't help but think, why don't you just prance your ass right on out here so I can finish these shitty jobs Adela assigned me?

"Come on, Mags. We must get ready for tonight unless you want to commit social suicide and stay here with this.... This—"

"Nobody?" I finish for her, which only garners a scathing glare from the bitch, and what the hell is up with calling Maggie Mags? She hates nicknames, or at least that's what she always told me, but maybe she doesn't mind it coming from this inept a-hole since she is currently smiling at her.

"Are you coming, Mags?" Maggie looks from her to me; her decision doesn't seem that difficult as she drops her head and spins to follow Natashia out. Focusing my attention back on the task at hand, I practically jump out of my own skin when I hear a loud crash behind me. I spin just in time to watch Natashia knock another one of the floral arrangements I put together as a centerpiece to the floor. Her eyes dare me to say something. I am screaming my mantra in my head, yet I fear if she knocks another one of them off the table, I will not be able to keep my mouth shut. Hell, I am not entirely sure I will be able to stop myself from knocking her ass out. "You missed a spot."

"Oh, you miserable." I snap, throwing the cleaning supplies I'm holding down. The only thing that stops me from throttling this bitch is Maggie's pleading eyes.

Because of Natashia's mess, I barely finish everything on my list before I have to run up to take a quick shower. Adela would have my head if I tried to serve anyone smelling like sweat and cleaners. Sliding into the outfit she provided, I hustle downstairs to ensure everything is ready in the kitchen ahead of the guests showing up.

An hour after the Ball began, I had everyone served and most of the dishes cleared. Currently, I am tucked into a corner of the room, waiting for the next order to be bellowed or, in my case, glared in my direction.

Having a ringside seat to the festivities, I can't help but notice Natasha glaring at the blonde Brady has been seeing. Good thing the old adage 'if looks could kill' is just an expression, or this poor girl might actually be dead. Even though I have had a secret crush on Brady for years, I admit I'm doing a little happy dance watching Natashia lose her shit because he's ignoring her. Meanwhile, Brady, who by the way, looks amazing in his tailor-fitted black tuxedo, is completely oblivious to her tantrums.

His eyes meet mine, and I notice something flicker within them for the briefest second. My own uncertainty has me breaking eye contact first. After what I assume was a safe amount of time, I look back up to discover him laughing with the group of people he is talking with. His hand is resting low on the blonde's back, and I wish it were me standing there for a fleeting moment. Shaking the thought away, I am further pulled out of my daydream when I hear a snicker behind me. Travis, of freaking course, it has to be the only other person in the world I would prefer staying far, far away from.

"You really need to give up on that little fantasy of yours. It is never going to happen. Me on the other hand.... Well, let's just say I would be more than happy to help you scratch that little itch."

"I would sooner put my paw in a bear trap," I hiss.

"We could arrange it if you're into that kind of thing." He says, bringing his mount directly next to my ear as he runs a finger up my arm.

"Listen, asshole," I snap, but he cuts me off before I can finish.

"Ah—ah—ah, Shay, careful what you are about to say. After all, you wouldn't want my best friend and your wet dream to overhear you." His lips against my ear as he kisses me make my skin crawl. "Especially since he's watching right now." Again he slides his finger up my arm before he raises his glass, grinning at Brady, who merely shakes his head before walking away. I swear he looked mad about something; however, I have no idea what I could have done to piss off one of the leaders this time.

I glance around the room quickly, taking in where the other leaders are before I spin and snarl, "If you ever put your god damn hands on me again, you won't have hands left to touch anybody, including yourself."

Travis doesn't back off quite the contrary. He leans further into my personal space before muttering maliciously, "I look forward to breaking you, Shay."

Pushing him away from me, I storm into the kitchen to finish cleaning the mess. After I'm done, I fully intend on calling it a night. I think, no actually I know, I have had just about enough of this shit for one day.

Thirty minutes later, I'm back in my room, stripping off the ridiculous servant uniform I was made to wear tonight. On my way back to the quarters, I grabbed two beers. I think I more than deserve these, and since anyone who would care that I took them is currently boozing it up downstairs, I plan to enjoy every last drop before I fall into bed for the night. The only good thing about tonight is I found twenty bucks I can add to my minuscule savings. I open the first beer, taking a much-needed drink before making my way over to the loose floorboard under my desk to retrieve the money I have managed to save over the last three years. Six hundred fifty-seven dollars. Nothing to write home to mom about, but it's something at least.

The light knock on my door causes me to jump as I rush towards it without realizing I still hold the cash in my hand. Knowing I need to do something with it, I cram the money into the pocket of my jeans; I can put it back after I finish with whoever is here. I am completely baffled when I find Brady standing on the other side of the door. To say he looks pissed would be an understatement.

"What are you doing, Shay?"

Does he know about the money? I subconsciously place my thumb through the belt loop to ensure the money is not visible, but he never looks down, which tells me his impromptu visit has nothing to do with my hidden stash. Leaving only one other thing it could be; I figure he has to be mad because I left the Ball without saying anything to anyone. Resulting in my immediate attempt to justify my actions, "I thought I finished everything for the night. I apologize if I was still needed."

"What the hell are you talking about?" he yells. Clearly confused about what has him so pissed, I remain silent. "I should have listened when everyone tried to tell me, but no, I have to be some dumb fucking idiot."

"Brady, I don't have any idea—"

"No, you don't. Why, Shay, just tell me why."

"If you just tell me why you are so mad at me, I might be able to answer your question."

"Travis! Why are you fucking Travis?"

My eyes grow wide. Is he seriously suggesting what I think he's implying, "I'm not fucking anyone, least of all Travis."

"Bullshit. He told me everything."

"And you never stop to think he could be lying to you?"

"He has no damn reason to lie to me. You on the other hand," His eyes move over my frame, and again I see something flash in his eyes. If I didn't know better, I would say he's hurt, but that's just crazy.

"Why would I lie?"

"You seem to be doing it a lot lately."

"What the hell have I lied about, Brady?"

"You lied about being a thief."

"I didn't steal anything," I snap.

"Sure you didn't. Just like you didn't take the beer?" His eyes move to the bottle I mistakenly left sitting on my nightstand. Good thing the other one is sitting on the floor under my desk.

"You have got to be shitting me. Here take the damn thing." I tell him, stomping over to snatch the unopened bottle before I return to him, thrusting it into his hand.

"Tell your mom she can add it to my tab." I hope I was able to keep the hurt out of my voice. I can't believe this. I took two damn lousy beers, and as far as he knows, it was only one. For this, he is going to believe everything those two vile assholes have said about me.

Brady's eyes focus on me, making it easy to see that some of his anger has melted away. Raking his hand through his hair, he looks down at the beer I shoved in his hand. I shut the door, not wanting to be subjected to further accusations from him or anybody else tonight. I think I've heard everything I need to hear about what he does or does not believe about me.

He taps on my door again. Hell, I'm surprised he knocked. Since he practically owns this packhouse, including the room I stay in, he would have been well within his rights to kick down the door, but he didn't. After a minute, when I think he finally understands I have no intentions of opening it, he murmurs, "I'm sorry, Shay, I shouldn't...." He doesn't finish the sentence, and I hear him sit something down outside my door. I don't have to guess what it is; I know he left the beer sitting out there.

Standing in the middle of the room, I work to bring my erratic breathing back under control. I am just getting ready to turn off the lights and call it a day when another knock has me ripping the door open. I am fully prepared to give him a piece of my mind until I realize it's not Brady; it's Travis.

Episode Nine: Run

Shay

I HAD JUST managed to bring my pounding heart under control, but it ramps back up seeing him holding the bottle Brady left for me.

"Tsk—tsk, Shay. It seems your sticky fingers were at work again."

I can't help when I growl, "Fuck you, Travis."

"That is my plan."

His eyes slide down from mine, landing on my breast. My skin crawls as his tongue glides over his lips. Nothing about his demeanor puts me at ease, leaving only one thought to slam the door closed and lock it before he comes in here. There is no way he would risk breaking down the door. He would have to answer to the Alpha and Luna if he did that, and there is very little he would be able to accuse me of that would justify him destroying pack property.

Shoving the door with all my might, his hand darts out to stop it before I can get the damn thing closed. Throwing his shoulder against the partially open door causes it to slam into me. The impact sends me staggering back several feet; as a result, my hand loses contact with the door. Racing forward in an attempt to stop him from entering my room, he waits until I'm close enough; before he kicks it, the door flies open, and the corner hits my mouth, splitting my lip.

The feel of something wet running down my chin confirms he did significant damage. My only alternative now is to find something I can use as a weapon. The problem is he already has one, and he wasted no time slamming the beer bottle into the side of my head. The smack from the door is nothing compared to the impact from the bottle; as flashes of blinding white light blur my vision, I stumble back, colliding into the side of my bed, and end up toppling onto it. Before I can right myself, he's on me, holding me down as he paws at my shirt. I flail my arms hoping and praying they will come into contact with his head. My only thought is to knock him off balance; if I can get him off me enough, I can shift into my wolf. I stand a much better chance against him in my wolf's form than in my human one.

When my nail grazes his face, causing a slight nick to his right cheek, his eyes change from just icy to murderous. The explosion of pain racing through my head from his punch takes most of the fight out of me. I vaguely hear my wolf whimpering as she desperately tries to get me to fight back. She knows as well as I do that my only chance to survive this is to shift. His hand tightens painfully around my neck, and I realize this just morphed from a fight to stop whatever plans he had in mind to do to me to a fight for my life since my next actions may decide if I make it out of here alive and in one piece or not.

Every ounce of fear I felt when his hand ensnared my throat in his iron grip triples when he yanks my pants open. Oh my god, ohmygod, he's going to rape me.

Get up, Shay! My wolf is screaming through my head. *Move now*! Does she not understand I'm trying, but my limbs currently are not cooperating with my brain. His mouth smashes against mine as his hand dips into my jeans. I viciously bite his lower lip; he pulls his hand out of my jeans to deliver another blow. This time I turn my head just in time, so the impact is to the back of my head rather than my already severely damaged face.

"If you fucking do something like that again, I'll kill you, Shay," He snarls as he wipes the blood off his lip with the back of his hand. The hand around my throat clamps a little tighter, but it's enough to finally cut off the tiny breaths I previously could suck in. "Nod if you understand me."

I have no alternative other than to comply, praying he will release his grip enough to allow any amount of precious air to flood into my oxygen-starved lungs. As he fumbles to remove his pants, I see the only opportunity I may get. I wait until he is confident I have given up before slamming my head into the bridge of his nose as hard as possible. The attack results in another explosion of lights across my field of vision, but he gets the worst of it. As painful as it was for me, it had to be worse for him.

"Please, it must have been worse," I silently pray. With Travis momentarily distracted, I yank my knee up, and I land a direct hit to his groin, resulting in him immediately rolling off me to cradle his injured nose and manhood.

Not wasting any time, I bolt for the door. Taking the stairs three at a time, I make it to the ground floor when I hear the first growl coming from somewhere above me. As I bust through the back door, I begin stripping my clothes. I need to shift if I hope to make it out of this mess with my skin intact. I also realize that my actions tonight have officially made me rogue, so I need to keep my clothes, but I don't have anything to put them in. Forgoing the removal of my shirt, I figure my wolf may not be comfortable, and it may be ripped and stretched beyond recognition, but at least I would have a shirt to wear. The only other thing I have time to grab is my jeans which I tie around my waist before I drop into my wolf and race away from the pack house.

I make it twenty yards into the woods when I hear the first howl coming from somewhere behind me. It only takes a second before there is a response to his call, followed by a third and fourth. Fuck, he just mind-linked to the sentries. I cannot let any of them catch me; if they do, they'll return me to the packhouse, and I know if I go back into the only place I have ever called home, I will never walk out of there again. Travis will make sure of it.

My wolf picks up speed, sprinting through the night like Death himself is chasing us because that is precisely who's hunting us, Death in the form of a six-foot egotistical madman named Travis. So we run, no longer afraid of what will happen to us if we leave the pack. Those fears are a long-forgotten memory. Fear of staying and the brutal death that will inevitably befall me are the only things racing through my frenzied thoughts.

Branches slap against us, ripping large chunks of fur from my wolf. Yet she does not waiver, nor does she slow. I can still hear the calls of my former pack members calling out from somewhere behind me, but the howls are growing softer with each stride we take. I know the closest town I can hide in or even grab a bus is still ten miles away. But making it to Whitefish is my only hope to put as much distance between them and us as possible. I can only pray my wolf has enough stamina to make it there. I realize now all those early mornings I could have been in bed sleeping instead of exercising my wolf have paid off because had I done to my wolf what Nan did to hers, I would have collapsed long ago.

Even though I know I will regret this soon, I push my wolf to cut across the river rather than go around; this will cut two miles off my trip, not to mention it will erase my scent making it more difficult for the scouts to track me. Not allowing her to immediately exit the frigid river, I force her to swim upstream several hundred yards before allowing her to get out of the water, further exhausting my wolf.

An hour later, the first lights from Whitefish Montana come into view. I know I can catch a bus, but it only runs at certain times of the day, and since Whitefish is not very big, Travis will not have much problem spotting me. So I linger inside the woods until daybreak. My muscles are cramped from the cold air and my late-night forced swim. I need to go into town to find out when I can get the first bus out of here. I also need to buy a new shirt, sweatshirt or coat, and a pair of cheap shoes. It would probably be best to grab a couple bottles of water and a box of granola bars or something I can eat while I travel. As I stand here debating everything I need to do, a sickening thought occurs to me. What if the money I had in my pocket fell out during my escape through the woods? If I lost my money, I am totally fucked.

I shift back into my human form and take a deep breath before sliding my hand into my pocket. It's gone. Oh my goddess, I lost the only money I had. My heart sinks as I slump to the ground. For only the second time in my adult life, I feel my eyes brimming with completely useless tears. They are not going to help me out of this situation; they won't buy me a bottle of water, they can't buy me a pair of shoes or a shirt, and they sure as shit can't buy me a bus ticket out of this godforsaken town.

I know I only have one choice left after wallowing in my own misery for longer than I care to admit. Reaching my hand up, I allow my fingers to skim over the thin chain around my neck, the same chain holding the only thing I have left from my mom and dad, her engagement ring. I had to keep the ring hidden all these years so Adela would not take it from me. For a long time, it stayed safely tucked away under the loose floorboard in my room: however, after years of wearing the cheap chain, Adela quit asking about it, allowing me to hide the ring under my shirt. Normally when I shift, I leave the ring hidden in my room so I won't risk it slipping off my wolf form; thankfully, because I left my shirt on when I shifted last night, the chain remained tucked inside my shirt, so I did not lose it during my escape.

Resigning myself to what I have to do, I slide my hands across the ground, and I cannot believe my luck when I uncover some of my money buried under the leaves. I find several more loose bills while scurrying around on my hands and knees. It's not all of it, but most of it is here. I found just over four hundred dollars; this should be more than enough to get me the ticket and everything else I need. Straightening my damaged clothes as best I can, I take one final look around my surroundings before taking what I consider my first step toward my new life.

Now I just need to pray the pack isn't here looking for me.

Episode Ten: Ash Rock

Foster

"*I* SEE YOUR fan club gained another new member."

I don't have to look over my shoulder to know who Finch is talking about. The new barmaid Seamus hired, I think her name is Mandy, has made it obvious she's interested, but I'm not looking for anything right now. I come into town to have a few beers, shoot some pool, and relax. What I am definitely not looking for is someone to hook up with.

"You probably shouldn't keep bending over like that because her eyes are glued to that *perfect ass of yours*," Finch says the last part in the highest shrillest girliest voice he can manage.

"Shut up and pay attention to the table. I'm getting ready to kick your ass, and I would hate for you to miss it, jackass."

"Cuz you wound me."

I grin before taking my next shot, "Eight ball corner pocket." The ball sinks clean with the cue spinning back towards me.

"I don't know why I even try. Want another beer?"

"Sounds good. Am I racking?"

"Sure, but you're buying," He laughs as he snatches the money from my hand I am already holding out for him.

When the bar goes from a roaring party to a screeching halt, I know what happened; my buddy Atlas just walked in. He's the president of a local motorcycle club, and everyone tends to give him and his club a wide berth. I'm not sure why he and his vice president, Denver, are great guys. The person these people should be leery of, but the one they seem to welcome with open arms, is the local thug Maximus, who has his ass parked in the corner booth like some damn kingpin. He acts as if he cares for the people in this town and specifically the ones who patron this bar; the simple fact is Max doesn't give two shits about them, and I suspect he's the one behind many of the break-ins and brutal attacks plaguing this town over the last six months.

"Well-well-well, if it isn't the town stud."

"Don't believe the rumors," I mumble, glancing up at Atlas as I rack the balls. A booming laugh rips from Denver. The rest of the night, they decide to cut me a break. Four hours and several rounds of pool later, games I thoroughly kicked all their asses in; we are getting ready to leave when Mandy comes out to go home. The asshole Max and his five buddies are hot on her heels. I have no interest in the girl, but something about his demeanor and her body language stops me from leaving.

"Thanks, Max, but you don't have to walk me to my car."

"What kind of man would let a pretty little thing like you leave out of here at this hour by yourself?" He grabs her arm a little too aggressively. This asshole is used to getting what he wants, and it appears she has caught his attention. If the rumors are anything to go by, the last thing you want is to hook your star to him since he tends to beat the woman who does.

Worse, this miserable prick brags about it, like hitting a girl makes him a big man. As a result, I step under the light to make my presence known. The look of relief washing over her face tells me I made the right decision.

"It's okay, really. Foster's still here, so I'm not alone." Atlas nudges my shoulder, chuckling. I know it's because there are four of us standing out here, but this girl decided to single me out. Max's head snaps over in our direction. His eyes narrow when he realizes we're still standing here. It's no secret we don't like one another. I step forward, my wolf clawing to come out.

"Well, since knight in shining armor, or should I say mutt, is here, I guess I'll leave you to it." He turns, saluting me with his middle finger. This guy is such a fucking putz. Of course, the comment he made is a dig because he knows what very few people in this town know about me; I'm a shifter. I belong to the large pack in Colorado; we occupy most of the lands Northeast of this town. He knows this because he stumbled across me when I shifted back to my human form after going for a run twelve months ago. But I know something about him, also something he manages to hide better than any other one I have met before; he's a rogue. How he has been able to hide his wolf from the other wolves in the area and the humans around him is a mystery making him extremely dangerous since he could expose my pack and me.

Max focuses on me while his passenger flashes a gun as they drive by. Atlas takes a step closer to me. I appreciate his action, but I'm not worried about Max or any of his gang. His nose twists up, causing the scowl already settled on his face to increase. While the three of us are all business, my cousin Finch is being his typical jokester self when he steps forward, waving enthusiastically at them. I am aware he only did it to further piss Max off, which has Atlas, Denver, and me roaring with laughter.

When Finch and I return home, I decide to crash at my aunt Clair's place rather than risk waking the entire pack. Aunt Clair still keeps a room at her house for me even though I moved into the packhouse over a year ago. She told me I could stay while I began renovating the cottage I bought, but I no longer wanted to take advantage of her generosity. She's already taken care of me long enough. Besides, I should have my place ready soon. It's not much, just a small three-bedroom little cottage down by the lake, but it's mine. Which is something I have never been able to say before. Aunt Clair took me in right after my mom died, and while she has always treated me like one of her own pups, I never felt like the house was mine. Not like you do when you live with your parents. Don't get me wrong, my aunt is great, and I love her and my two cousins more than they will ever know; I would just really like to have something I can call my own.

The next morning I get up early to cook everyone breakfast, a tradition I started a long time ago and continue anytime I'm here on a Saturday morning.

"Oh, my goddess, have I missed this," my other cousin and Finch's twin Vanessa, or Ness as we call her, declares as she comes in and plops down on the chair at the table.

"Breakfast will be done soon, but the coffee is ready now if you want some."

"You are the best damn cousin a girl can ask for." I laugh as I flip the pancake catching it easily.

"Close your mouth Lindsey," Ness says, and I can hear the exasperation in her tone. While we were growing up, Ness hated bringing her friends home. She always said she never knew if they wanted to hang out with her or ogle Finch and me. As suspected, when I look over my shoulder, I discover Ness's best friend staring at me with her mouth open.

"You know Foss, they make these things called shirts. You should look into them," Ness declares while shoving Lindsey's mouth closed.

Before I can respond, Finch bounces into the room catching Ness in a headlock before he kisses the top of her head, declaring, "And miss seeing reactions like hers."

Lindsey's face goes from red to radioactive in a matter of seconds when she realizes we all caught her staring. Finch is wearing even less than I am since he just has on a pair of shorts, and now this poor girl doesn't know where to look, so she settles on the ceiling when I sit the plate of pancakes on the table.

"Do either one of you know what clothes are," Ness's screech causes a booming laugh from both of us while Lindsey continues to inspect the ceiling. Of course, Finch can't let it go, so he leans over to examine the space Lindsey is concentrating on.

"Something up there?"

"No, dumbass, she's trying to avoid looking at you two dipshits." Ness's response causes this poor girl's face to turn an alarming shade of purple.

"Oh, sweetheart, I don't mind. Stare away. Me and my boy here don't mind gaining the attention of a pretty little thing like you." I want to tell him to leave me out of his comments, but I feel bad when she drops her head on the table.

"Alright, don't be an asshole; leave her alone," I say as I throw a pancake at him. He catches it, shoving the whole thing in his mouth.

"Yeah, Finch, don't be an asshole," Ness reiterates. Finch pretends he's locking his mouth, then tosses the key over his shoulder before he winks at Lindsey, causing Ness to hit him in the back of his head.

"Don't be a jerk, jerk!"

The rest of the morning is filled with light conversation, just like it used to be until Ian shows up. Ian is the beta of our pack but not by choice; he despises the Alpha and continually asks me why I didn't take the role after I defeated the last Alpha. I only did it to protect Ness and the rest of the pack. He was a total asshole who thought the female pack members should be at his beck and call. I showed him the error of his ways, and when I turned down the role of Alpha, his inept cousin claimed it. While Deacon is nowhere near as bad as Andre was, he just doesn't know the first thing about running or protecting this pack.

"Damn, it's been months since I had Saturday morning breakfast," Ian declares, clapping his hands together. I know he came over to see my aunt. Finding me here is just an added bonus, and I'll give him a count of five before he asks me the same question he always does. Five, four, three, two....

"So when you gonna take your rightful place, Foster?" And there it is. I merely laugh as I hand him a plate.

Episode Eleven: Cashier And A Prayer

Shay

I HAVE NEVER been more nervous in my entire life. I fully expect one of the pack members to pop out from around the corner any second, and it's not like I'm inconspicuous here or anything. My long blonde mane is not hard to miss, not to mention my shirt is stretched out and torn in several places; if this wasn't enough, I'm not wearing any shoes. Hell, I'm practically a walking billboard with a flashing arrow pointing at four words: Shifter on the run.

Lucky for me, I find a general store open, allowing me to grab a couple articles of clothes, a hooded jacket, a pair of shoes, and some snacks. First, I slip on the fresh shirt before putting on the jacket and pulling the hood up to hide my hair.

The clerk watches me intently but doesn't ask any questions, at least not until I duck down to hide behind the counter when

I see Travis and three other pack members just outside the store. The older man leans across the counter to stare down at me, but before he can say anything, the jingle of the bell over the door pulls his attention. Without looking, I crawl around the counter to hide in the next checkout lane. Which is currently closed due to the lack of customers. Pressing myself against the counter, I try to make myself as small as possible.

My only saving grace is they cannot shift into their wolf forms; if they were able, then there is absolutely no way they wouldn't be able to smell me over here. While a shifter's sense of smell is heightened compared to our human counterparts, it is not as good as our wolf, and because of my late-night swim, staying out in the woods all night, and the new clothes, I pray it's enough to mask my scent.

"Mornin', gentlemen," The clerk greets the new arrivals with as much enthusiasm as he did when I came in. I don't have to guess who he is speaking to; I know it's my previous pack members.

"Have you seen this girl," Travis snaps. No one must have explained to him that you catch more flies with honey. Hopefully, his prickly personality will rub this guy the wrong way because if he tells them I'm over here, I'm as good as dead.

"Yeah, she was here." My heart seizes hearing him say this.

"Is she still here?"

"Nope. She came into the store right after I opened this mornin'." I have to force myself not to let out the breath I have been holding since they walked in. I think this guy might actually be trying to help me.

"Did you see where she went?"

"Can't say for sure. I can tell you the truck she left in was headin' east."

"Was she driving?"

"No, caught a ride with a trucker passin' through." Movement catches my attention, and I look up. I can barely see the top of Travis's head from my vantage point, but if he leans forward even a little bit, there is no way he won't see me.

"East you say, huh?"

"Ah, yep, from what I remember, they were headin' east."

"How long ago was this?" One of the other pack members named James asks.

"Is this girl in trouble or somethin'?"

"She stole a bunch of money, among other things." I listen to the welcome sound of Travis walking back toward the clerk.

"I hate thieves." Oh, my goddess. If he thinks I stole and they are merely trying to recover their lost possessions will he change his mind and tell them where I am?

"As most people do. So do you know what time she left in that truck?"

The clerk does not immediately respond, and with every passing second, my heart sinks, knowing he is going to tell them where I am any second now.

"Liars too. You know what I say, well I reckon you don't, so I'm gonna tell you, son. Thieves and liars are despicable individuals. Honestly, I'm not sure which one I dislike more."

"Is that so?"

"It is. Do you wanna know where that girl is?" I look around, desperate to find any means of escape as my heart ramps up from the flood of adrenaline coursing through my veins.

"I wouldn't have asked if I didn't really, *really* want to know." I can hear the irritation increasing in his tone, and I know the instant the cashier tells him where I am, he is going to pounce on me in full force. I am just preparing to jump up and take off running when the cashier continues.

"I overheard that trucker say somethin' about New York. They left bout forty-five minutes ago. If y'all hurry, I'm pretty damn sure you can catch that miserable S.O.B. lying thief." WTF just happened? When I do not hear them leaving, I wonder if they know the cashier lied. I wait with bated breath, praying he will not want to risk me getting too far away from him.

"Thanks." This is the clipped show of gratitude he will be offering this man. What an asshole. I don't let out the breath I have been holding until I hear the door shut. Dropping my head down on my knees, I work to bring my ragged breath, racing heart, and shaking hands back under control.

"Now, don't you get up yet, young lady. They're still standin' right outside the store," He mumbles. I want to tell him no worries there since I'm not sure my legs will support my weight right now. "You see that door over yonder?"

"Yes," I whisper.

"You go on inside my office and wait. I'll just make sure he leaves, and then I'll come to get ya. Now I know this may not be dignified and all, but you can't stand up just yet. You're gonna hafta crawl in there. Okay?"

"Yes, sir." I complied with his request; after all, I don't have too many other options right now. When I get into his office, I am suddenly struck with how bad of an idea this was coming in here. If Travis returns and decides he wants to check the store, I have no means of escape from this room. Shit—shit—shit! How could I be so stupid? I briefly contemplate going back into the store until I hear muffled voices and cannot tell if it's Travis or not. Diving under the desk, I pull the chair in as far as I can and pray if he searches in here, he will not find me hiding under the desk.

I remain in my hiding spot, counting off each second when five minutes have elapsed, the door opens, "He left."

I slowly climb out from under the desk and cautiously peek over it. When I realize he's standing there alone, I stand up before acknowledging what he just did for me, "Thank you."

"Well now, I meant what I said. I hate thieves and liars—"

"I didn't st—" he holds his hand up to silence me before I finish.

"I don't know if you are or ain't a thief, and I imagine if you did take somethin' of that fellers, it's cuz he isn't the best sorta chap. One thing I know for certain is that he's a damn liar. Now I know you don't know me from Adam, but you wanna tell me what's goin' on, young lady?"

I know I can't tell him what I am or about the pack, so I tell him as close to the truth as possible, "He wants me to...." I am having a hard time coming up with something I can say to this man about why Travis wants me, so I hope my deliberate omission will lead him to believe Travis just wants me for sex. "And I don't want to. Don't want to be with someone like him."

"Is he the one that put those bruises and cuts on your face?" Shit, I didn't even think about what my face must look like right now. At least this time, when I answer, it's not a half-truth.

"Yes."

" I take it you snuck into town hoping to catcha bus outta here?"

"Yes."

"Where are you goin'? You gotta plan in place?"

"Not really. Just as far away from here as I can get."

"Do ya got money for bus fare?"

"I have a little."

"Well, now I know it ain't much," he pulls his wallet out and tries to hand me some cash.

"I can't take your money; it wouldn't be right."

"I figured you say that. I knew that S.O.B. was lying bout you being a thief. Now you go on and take it. You're gonna need money to buy food, and I sent them fools east, so you make sure the bus you take goes in any direction but that one." This time he doesn't wait for me to take the cash electing to shove it into my jacket pocket instead. "And here I made you a little somethin'. I put water, chips, and a few other snacks you can eat while on the road. Sorry I don't have anythin' else I can give ya."

"You've already done more than enough…. Thank you."

"Now you go on over; the greyhound should be comin' through soon, and if there isn't a bus leavin' for a while, you come back around here, and you can wait until it's time for you to go."

Before he lets me leave, he walks outside, chatting with several people who walk by. When he is confident Travis is nowhere near, he waves me out. Pulling the hood up again, I scurry towards the bus station. As nervous as I was coming into town this morning, I am terrified now, and my uncontrolled racing heart proves it. The only bus route not heading east that I can afford is towards Colorado. I don't want to be in a large town; a small one is better for my wolf, and it has to have space I can release her, so I make my choice, purchase the ticket and board the bus. Once settled in, I pull the money he gave me out of my pocket and count close to a hundred dollars.

"Shay?"

Episode Twelve: Rogue

Brady

I CANNOT BELIEVE I ever trusted her. How anyone could steal the money we collected at the Harvest Ball is beyond me; everyone knows what this money is used for. Without it, I have no idea how in the hell we will keep the hospital that serves the five packs surrounding it up and running. Not to mention how we will continue to pay for the treatment of the young pups who develop a rare brain cancer that only seems to affect wolf shifters. First a necklace, then the booze, and the icing on her shit cake was the hospital fund. Goddess only knows if she took anything else.

I am such a fucking idiot. I managed to convince myself this chick was simply misunderstood. Hell, I all but told my dad we treated her like shit and we should be ashamed of ourselves. I guess this just further proves I have a lot to learn. Maybe dad shouldn't declare me as the next alpha of the pack. If I can't even detect when someone is pulling the wool over my eyes or differentiate between good and bad, what kind of leader can I ever be to my pack?

I am so pissed at Travis for not getting me and my dad the second he discovered her taking the money, but no, he decided to go after her with only two sentries. Had he come to dad or me, we could have had the entire pack out looking for her. She would have never made it off our lands and certainly would not have left with the funds.

I have no idea why dad made me stay here to coordinate while everyone else is out looking for her. I guess this is his way of punishing me for not listening to him all these years regarding Shay. Either that or he was just afraid I would feel sorry for her and let her go. I can assure you this will never happen. She didn't care about the wolves who depend on that hospital or the pups whose lives hang on the balance of the research we fund with that money, so why would I care about someone this fucking selfish?

She took close to a million dollars, a million fucking dollars. Every time I think about it, my blood boils. I want to be out there looking, not sitting in here on my ass fielding god damn phone calls. My dad's idea was to split up, to send half the pack up north and east while the other half went to the south and west. I tried to tell my dad she would run straight into Whitefish, hoping to get a bus, but he was so furious he refused to listen.

Pacing around the room, Travis has kept in contact with me this whole time, but I haven't heard anything from my dad or his beta. When my phone rings, I jerk it up only to discover Maggie's name on the screen. I hope she is calling to inform me she found her and not just to check in.

Shay

I whip my head up only to discover Maggie standing by me. This time my heart doesn't just race. It pounds so hard and so fast that I can feel it through my entire body. Adrenaline releases into my bloodstream as my fight-or-flight response kicks in. My eyes flick towards the window, terrified I will find Travis standing outside the bus waiting for me to depart.

"Shay, you have to come with me."

"I can't do that, Maggie," I mutter.

"Tobias and Adela are furious that you stole all the donation money from the fall harvest. They are demanding you be brought back to answer the allegations."

"You can't believe...."

"Just tell me where the money is, Shay."

"First thing Maggie, I didn't steal anything. Second, they want to crucify me. They could give a shit less what I have to say. Travis made that shit up because I ran from him after he tried to rape me in my room last night. Third, if I go back there, either Adela or Travis or possibly both will make sure I never walk out of there again, and I'm somewhat partial to living. So I can't go back with you."

"Travis told everyone he caught you red-handed, and when he confronted you, you hit him and took off."

"Of course he did. Do you really think he would tell the Alpha and Luna he tried to rape me, and I rejected him?"

"Why would he need to rape anyone? He has girls falling all over him." Her response has enough bite to tell me she doesn't believe me.

I can't tell you how much it hurts knowing the only person I have ever called a friend doesn't believe me. She believes a low-life piece of shit who has picked on her most of her life instead of me. Yanking my hood off, I snap,

"Do you think I did this to myself? Did I punch myself in the face, split my lip, choke myself? Yeah, I can see where *the pack* would think I did some crazy shit like that." The emphasis on the pack is so she understands I now count her among the ones who could give a shit less if I live or die. Well, until they want something cleaned or breakfast, lunch, or dinner, especially since Nan can't deliver on it, maybe I'm part of the pack.... Nope, I take that back. Not even then am I considered to be a part of their pack.

Maggie's eyes grow wide while she takes in the damage. Her hand flies to her mouth before she tentatively reaches out to touch my face. On instinct, I jerk away. To be honest, I have had enough unwanted physical contact to last me a lifetime, and she no longer gets to pretend she's my friend. Not any more. This time when she speaks, it's much softer, "If you just come back, Shay, we can get this worked out. We'll tell the Alpha and Luna—"

"No, Maggie. I'm not going back. You have two choices here you can either step off the bus and pretend like you never found me, or you can call whoever the hell you're supposed to report to and tell them where I am. Regardless I promise you I am not getting off this bus, and if they come for me, I will not go down without a fight."

Without waiting for her response, I pull my hood up again to cover my face and sit back in my seat. I refuse to look at her any longer, not now, not after knowing she could believe the lies Travis spewed about me. It's too late to make any changes to my ticket. I'll have to figure out how far I can travel once I arrive in Colorado. I can just make out her reflection in the window, and my heart sinks when I realize she is holding her phone now. My heart falls as I watch her make the call.

"Hi, Brady. Yeah, I'm at the bus station right now." It looks like my new adventure, much like my life, is over before it ever really began.

I can make out bits and pieces of his clipped reply, ".... she there?"

I know she is looking directly at me through the reflection in the window. She begins taking several small breaths; I listen to each one as she exhales it like the countdown of a timer. This one is counting down the seconds I have left in my life. I think about my mom and dad and wonder if I will see them again. After what feels like an eternity, she sighs before answering, "No. She's not here."

My head snaps in her direction, but she isn't looking at me. She seems defeated with her eyes closed and her head dropped. Brady is giving her directives regarding where she should go next. After she hangs up with Brady, she does not say anything else to me. Maggie merely turns to exit the bus before going over to sit on the bench. I know she is battling with following the orders of Tobias and Adela, but I can also see the internal war brewing within her, knowing I'm right. I think, for the first time ever, she realized if she had told them where to find me, she would be effectively signing my death warrant.

As the bus door slides shut and she slips her phone into her pocket, I know she has made her choice. She may change her mind. She may still make the call and tell them at the last second that I jumped on a bus heading to Colorado; however, right here.... Right now. She has decided to give me a chance. One I will not squander. As the bus begins to pull away, her head lifts, and I can see the unshed tears shining in her eyes. I slowly raise my hand, acknowledging the girl I have called a friend my entire life and what she just did for me.

This is also when I realize I am officially a *Rogue*.

Episode Thirteen: Colorado

Shay

*H*AVING NEVER LEFT the pack before, I have to admit I'm antsy and excited all rolled into one. I am anxious because I have never been off pack land, so I have no idea what to expect. Excited because, once again, I have never been away from pack land, and there are so many magnificent and beautiful things to see. I find my eyes glued to the scenery as it flashes by outside the window. I also watch the people in the cars we pass. Living their life, laughing, loving one another, and just being a family. I feel like an interloper when I watch too long, inserting myself into their peaceful family moment. Others are not so friendly; one car we pass has a lady screaming at the top of her lungs about how he, I assume he is her husband, never lets her buy anything she wants. He calmly tells her she already has five other pairs of black heels; he doesn't understand why she needs yet another pair. This takes her already shrill voice to a whole new level; I never knew a woman's voice could go that

Marcelle Valentine

high. I try to hide my amusement when he turns to look at me, but I lose the battle when he rolls his eyes. Grinning, I lift my hand in a show of sympathy.

"Are you even listening to me?" She screeches as she leans over to see what has his attention.

"Yes, dear." Not wanting to get the guy in any more trouble, I sink down in my seat, laughing.

It's crazy how different this world is from the one I have lived in my entire life. If I was back at the pack house, I would be cleaning one room or another while getting ready to make lunch for the whole pack. But out here, people are just living life. A car full of girls around my age comes by. They are all laughing while singing along with the music, and I suddenly realize this is how life should have been all along; I also realize this is the life Natashia has had. Spending time with your friends, making corny jokes, talking about boys you think are handsome, and this thought alone makes my heart squeeze, realizing precisely how much life I have actually missed out on.

Five hours later, we finally arrived in Colorado. I depart the bus, not having the first clue of what I will do. Sense tells me staying in a large city would better hide me, but nervous energy demands I find something smaller. Besides, my lack of funds would seriously cut into my being able to find some place to stay, at least any place I would feel safe doing it. Not to mention living in a big city will not allow me to release my wolf. No, I need to move into one of the smaller towns surrounded by trees and woods. I won't have to worry about food. I can hunt small game to feed myself, but I still need some place to stay, and I imagine a room will be much cheaper in a small town. Which is how I find myself standing on the edge of the property for another pack of wolf shifter's territory.

I have no intention of joining another pack; hell, they would probably laugh me off their lands, but being close to one brings a certain peaceful calm while reminding me of what I am, rogue. And one thing I know is pack wolves have no use for rogues, so I'll also have to be careful. Giving their land a wide berth, I end up in a small town not far from the pack. I just hope they don't realize what I am if they come into this town.

The town I end up in has a population of just over 10,000 residents, big enough to hide among them yet small enough to hopefully not draw the attention of my pack if they come looking for me. Okay, the town I plan to settle in has been selected. Now I need to find a job, some place to stay, and lord almighty, I need a shower. Deciding to splurge for two nights, I get a room at the cheapest motel in town. After that, I don't know what I'm going to do because I am running out of money fast.

After going out and applying for jobs at several different places, I stopped at the only establishment close to the hotel that offers food, a bar named Stooges. The parking lot has a few cars scattered around, but it's not packed, so I don't feel completely out of place when I walk in. Selecting a stool at the far end of the bar away from everyone else, I am greeted by an overweight older man who reminds me of Santa Claus; if Santa had long red hair, he wore pulled back in a ponytail.

"Welcome to me bar, names Seamus. What can I do ya for?"

"Ummm...." I hesitate, not really sure how to answer him.

"He means what can he get for you."

"Oh, I was hoping I could get a burger and something to drink."

"Aye, sure." He tells me as he ambles back towards the kitchen.

"You would think after all these years he would speak better English," the man who helped translate yells more to Seamus than me. "His Irish roots come out the more he drinks, and today has been a dandy."

"Bollocks," Seamus shouts from the kitchen, followed by several pans crashing to the ground somewhere on the other side of the door.

"Is he going to be okay in there?" I quietly ask.

"Yeah, he can be ripped roaring and still cook a mean burger. Isn't that right, you ol' codger?"

"Houl yer whisht, bloody muppet." I have no idea what the hell he said, but it has the man who has been talking to me howling with laughter.

"Names Hyde."

"Nice to meet you; I'm Shay."

"New in town?"

I'm not fully comfortable with all his questions, but at the same time, I don't want to draw attention to myself by making a big deal about it, so I just nod my head.

"What brings you to our neck of the woods?"

"Change of scenery," I reply just as Seamus brings my burger out and sits it in front of me.

"I got that. Put it on my tab."

"Oh, I can't—"

"Nonsense, it's my way of saying welcome to the neighborhood."

"Thank you."

"You want a wee half'n'?"

I smile, raising my shoulders, completely lost in what he just asked, "Beer, wine, whiskey."

"Oh, a beverage."

"Yay, that's what me said a wee half'n'."

"Sure, I'll take a beer."

"Any kind."

"I'll have what he's having."

After finishing my food, I notice Seamus doesn't seem to have any help. I'm not sure if they don't come in until later or if they called off. Regardless Seamus is busy enough he hasn't been able to bus the tables yet, and since Hyde and Seamus provided me with a welcome to the neighborhood lunch, I decided to repay him by busing the tables for him. While he is cooking for another patron, I quickly clear the dishes from the table and bar, wiping everything down and stacking the plates neatly in the bus bin. With the arrival of two more customers, Hyde gets their beers while I take their orders for food.

"Aye, what's this?"

"Well, it seems our new friend wanted to thank you for your generosity," Hyde says, winking at me.

"You didn't have to do that."

"And you and Hyde didn't need to give me lunch, but you did." I grin as I gather my stuff to leave.

"Don't be a stranger," it seems Seamus must be sobering up because while his Irish accent still comes through, I can understand him much better than I could when I first came in.

Back towards the door, I grin while responding, "Since you two are the only ones I know in this town, I will definitely—" My words are cut off when I run into someone coming into the bar.

"Oh my gosh, I am so sorry," spinning to face whoever I just ran into, I realize it was a guy coming in with four of his buddies.

"You can bump into me anytime." Something in his response and how he says it has my skin crawling, much like it did when

Travis talked to me. Pushing my hair behind my ear, I try to extract myself from his grip, but he refuses to remove his hands from my hips. Taking another step back, he takes one forward. "Don't break my heart and tell me you're leaving already?"

"Umm…. I am. Once again, I apologize I ran into you."

"Well, the least you can do to make it up to me is let me buy you a drink."

"Not really sure how that's making it up to you if you're the one paying."

"The pleasure of your company."

"Thanks, but I can't. Maybe another time."

"Now, don't be like that. What's your name, sweetness?"

"I really need to get going."

"Let her go." His eyes flick towards Hyde. Contempt and fury flash in them for a fleeting second. I hear movement behind me, and with a quick glance over my shoulder, I find Hyde is now standing. Before his eyes settle back on me, leaning down so his face is in line with mine, I am starting to realize this guy and Travis are two peas in a pod.

"What are you going to do, big man?" He may be talking to Hyde, but his eyes are focused solely on me.

"Aye, Max, the lady said she needs to go." This time it is Seamus's booming voice. Either Seamus is someone you do not mess with, or this guy just decided he didn't want to piss off the owner of the only bar in town. Because he quickly releases me, raising his hands in the air and taking several steps away from me.

"No harm, no foul sweetness." Something tells me this guy is going to be nothing but trouble.

Episode Fourteen: Pack Issues

Foster

*A*FTER IAN'S REPEATED request for me to take over as the pack leader, I decided to look into what the hell Deacon is doing that has him so hell-bent about this subject again all of a sudden. Ian always wanted me to take the Alpha position, which is partly why I challenged the last Alpha to begin with.

If Andre had just accepted his fate, he would no longer be our pack leader; however, he would still be alive. It is customary when an Alpha is challenged, and they lose the new leader normally doesn't permit the old Alpha to live. Ending the old Alpha's life is something I never truly agreed with, but even I have to admit it does reduce friction within the pack. Andre would not accept he was no longer the Alpha and continually challenged me, which was fine. I had no issues kicking his ass every day; until he went after Ness, it was then I realized I had to stop him. During our final fight, he told me he would never accept it and would make it his mission in life to make mine miserable. If this meant attacking my family, then so be it. It wasn't even so much what he said; it was the look in his eyes that settled it for me. I knew I only had one option; this was to take his life before he took the life of someone I loved.

After I killed Andre, I still had no desire to lead the pack; as I have stated before, it was never about me gaining power for myself; it was more about putting it right within the pack. When I removed Andre, the tradition states any wolf who wants the position can fight for it; the last man standing is awarded the title. Deacon won by pure chance. He certainly is not the best candidate.

I stayed at my house last night because I was working on renovation until late. Finch keeps telling everyone I am having an end-of-the-season bash there before it gets too cold; subsequently, I need to finish it since October has already come and gone. I should be heading into work instead of towards the pack house. Our pack runs the biggest construction company in the state. As one of the lead supervisors, I should be there helping my guys finish this huge contract, not checking into the dealings of our pack leader.

"Hey, Foster, I didn't expect to see you here." Betsy is a sweet girl who had a crush on me for a while until my best friend Archer came to hang out with me, and now she's only got eyes for him. Archer is a member of our sister pack, Whispering Winds, and he is just about the best guy I know, next to Finch, of course.

"Where's Deacon?"

"He left about thirty minutes ago and said he would be gone most of the day."

"What's he like? I mean working for him, what is he like?"

Betsy has to visibly force herself to swallow while her eyes dart around the office.

"It's okay, Bets; you don't have to say anything else."

When I turn to enter his office, she quietly tells me, "You worked so hard to remove one tyrant only to have another step into the role."

As I close the door to begin looking into his dealing, the only thought swirling through my mind is, "Well, shit."

*****

Brady

It's been three days since Shay slipped away with money meant for something important to this pack and several others. We have searched everywhere with no signs of her anywhere; it's like she just vanished. Of course, I realize Shay didn't disappear. While wolf shifters are many things, a magician is not one of them.

She is definitely not anywhere in this area which leads me to believe she left by bus, and the way Maggie has been acting, I am beginning to question if she did see Shay boarding a bus in town. I don't share my suspicions with anyone else because I don't want Maggie to take Shay's place within the pack. Even if Shay betrayed us, I understand why Maggie tried to protect her; they have been friends for a long time. Maggie didn't do anything so grievous to merit being treated like Shay was.

I shared my thoughts with my dad, Travis, and dad's beta Owen; they all said I didn't know what I was talking about. I have to admit I'm confused. Do they all think she is stupid? Let me put that shit to bed right now; the girl is not stupid, nor is she foolish or reckless. She knows what will happen to her once we find her. If these three want to bury their head in the sand and keep looking within a hundred miles of our pack land, so be it. I'll look into this on my own.

To start, I need to have a conversation with Maggie; if she did see her it might be possible she can tell me what bus Shay left on, and once I know the bus, I can figure out where it traveled to. If I stole close to a million dollars, I would want to get as far away from the rightful owner as possible. I know there were four buses she could have left on.

I find Maggie with Natashia and Sadie, which is the worst-case scenario if I want to get Maggie to talk. Natashia still thinks we are going to end up together. I can't stop the rush of air escaping me, knowing there is no way around this.

"Maggie, can I have a word with you?"

"Brady, where have you been hiding? It feels like it's been forever since we saw one another."

"I've been busy. Maggie, are you free?" Natashia leaps to her feet, practically knocking Maggie on her ass so she can get to me first.

"I am. I can help you with whatever you need."

"No. I need Maggie for this." Placing my hand out to help Maggie up, I hear a low growl coming from Natashia. I don't have time for this shit, and when Maggie hesitates, I reach down and pull her off the chair. I can feel Natashia and Sadie's eyes tracking us the entire way across the room.

Entering an empty office, I close the door before asking what I need to know, "First off, I want you to know this conversation is strictly between us." Maggie shifts as her eyes begin to dart around the room. "Maggie, I need to ask you something, and I need you to tell me the truth. Did you see Shay the day she disappeared?"

Maggie doesn't answer, but the deer in the headlight look she gives me tells me everything I need to know, "Maggie, I need you to tell me what bus she left on."

The look of terror overshadowing her features confirms she knows the answer to this question too.

Episode Fifteen: New Beginnings

Shay

*O*LD HABITS ARE hard to break. This is my prevailing thought as I watch the first rays of dawn coloring the sky. If I were back at the pack house, I would be on my way back from my morning run to begin cooking breakfast for everyone. Thinking about this makes me think of Nan. I wonder if they dumped everything on her after I left. I hate the thought of Nan being mistreated, even though she had no issues leaving everything for me to do. As fucked up as this may sound, I think of her as the grandmother I never had. My heart hurts a little, knowing I may never see her again.

I didn't sleep well last night; it was too quiet. I'm used to pack life, and someone was always coming or going. Not to mention it was not uncommon to have someone banging on my door in the middle of the night to wake me up when they needed something. I think the quiet will be the hardest thing I have to get used to.

Once the sun has risen enough to chase away the shadows from the night, I know what I have to do. The first thing is to find a job. Next, find a place to live and finally begin living the life I deserve. With my plan in place, I start the next phase of my life, a life free from servitude, free from fear, and free from a pack that didn't want me to begin with.

"Yeah, I got this shit. New life, new chances, new me," I say aloud to the empty room before I blow the hair out of my face. "Or I go broke, end up homeless and alone for the rest of my life. Yay me."

Five hours later, I am starting to think the whole homeless thing could become a reality. Wondering into Stooges, I need a drink and something to eat, and I could stand to see a friendly face, so here's hoping Seamus and Hyde are here tonight.

I admit I'm really happy when I see Hyde sitting in here, and I hear Seamus cussing from the kitchen while some drunk guy keeps bellowing he needs another drink.

"Shut up and stop being an arse. I am doing the best I can." Realizing Seamus is, for lack of a better word, ass-deep in the weeds between running the kitchen and the bar, I cross the invisible barrier between customer and barmaid to get the asshole another draft beer.

"How much sugar?" Looking over at Hyde with my eyes wide, he mouths two-fifty.

"Two dollars and fifty cents."

The drunk guy hiccups before he replies, "Keep the change." My eyes flick over to Hyde, who gives me a thumbs up. I lay the five dollars on the counter next to the cash register and turn to sit on the other side of the bar when Hyde and two other patrons place their drinks on the bar's ledge. Raising my shoulder, Hyde whispers,

"This means we're ready for another drink." My mouth gapes slightly open as I nod my head. Moving to get each person another drink, Hyde helps me out by signaling with his fingers how much I should collect from each person. Thankfully no one needed change. After everyone is served, I sit on the stool next to Hyde and wait for Seamus to get me a drink. When he comes storming out of the kitchen with a tray of food his mouth falls open seeing everyone sitting there contently having their drinks.

"Hey, what happened out here?"

Another hiccup from the drunk guy before he slurs, "Your new girl." Promptly followed by another hiccup.

"What are you about? What new girl?" The drunk guy points at me before giving a little wave with his fingers and a beaming drunken smile, promptly followed by another hiccup. Oh shit, busted.

"I apologize, Seamus. I shouldn't have just gone behind the bar without your permission. I just saw how busy you were and wanted to help you out. I put all the money next to the register under the glass."

"You did this?"

"She jumped in and served all your customers with a smile on her face, I might add, which directly related to the extra cash you have lying over there. I've told you before, you ol' codger, to remove the snarl and add a smile if you want people to give you their hard-earned cash." To further drive home his point, he gives Seamus a beaming grin showing entirely too many teeth.

"And I told you before no one asked you, 'sides this is me smile." He glares at Hyde his expression never changes. I have to refrain from laughing out loud when I realize his smile seems to be the same as his scowl.

"As for you…." He levels his gaze on me, and suddenly I don't feel like laughing anymore. I can't tell if he's pissed or furious. Either way, it doesn't matter because I believe I just lost the only place in town where I feel comfortable. "You start tomorrow. Be here at five. Maggie should be back so she can show you what to do."

Holy shit, did I just get a job, like a real paying job? I can't contain the ever-broadening grin covering my face. Hyde nudges me when Seamus takes the tray of food over to the waiting table. This also means I just checked one of my to-do's off my list with only two more to go.

"Thank you, Hyde. You have no idea how much this means to me."

"The only thing I did was tell him the truth; you did everything else. Besides, when would I ever get to see your smiling face if you get a job somewhere else?"

"Oh man, I am so excited about having my first job. I always wanted one." I realize I just said entirely too much when I see his questioning expression as he tilts his head to the side and pulls his eyebrows together. Shit Shay, you have to think before you speak.

You should leave right now, get up and leave. My wolf warns. But I can't keep running. I am almost out of money, not to mention I would have to be an idiot to walk away from the first and only job that has ever been offered to me.

"Shay?" Damn, the whole time I have been sitting here debating what I should do, Hyde has been watching me, making this entire interaction so much worse. I know I have to tell him something; there is no way in hell he will let this go, so I tell him what I hope will sufficiently explain why this is my first job while not exposing myself in the process.

"I had an extremely strict family."

"Crazy families, they're the worst."

"Tell me about it." Okay, I think I may have just pulled my ass out of the hole I dug.

We'll have to watch him in the future until we're sure. My wolf has calmed some, but I can still feel her scratching for me to release her. She's afraid for me more than she is for herself, and knowing this makes me love her even more.

I ordered a chicken sandwich for dinner. Of course, Seamus refused to let me pay. He also supplies me with more than one cocktail, which causes my head to swim. Let me tell you, the sandwich Seamus made for me tonight was even better than the burger yesterday, and it was pretty damn amazing, if I say so myself, but this could be because of the booze. Then again, I wonder if a shit sandwich would taste great since I am not the one who had to make it. This thought causes a little chuckle to escape me, resulting in Hyde's questioning expression again. This time I just shrug my shoulders while I give him a beaming smile.

After helping Seamus get through a rush of customers, I bid Hyde, the drunk guy who I found out is Jerry and happens to be a staple here at Stooges, and Seamus goodnight. I gather my stuff to head back to the hotel to look for another place to live since I will lose this room the day after tomorrow. Unless the tips here are amazing, I don't think I can afford another night there. Just like last night, as I am leaving, I run into some random guy. At least this one doesn't make my skin crawl. No, quite the opposite; he ignites every cell in my body as my wolf snaps to attention.

"Excuse me." His eyes linger on me, and I see something flash within them as they dilate. He drops his hand, quickly looking away before he moves further into the bar. The loss of his hand on my arm has my wolf whimpering. My heart rate amps up, sending blood rushing to my extremities. And the only thought I can register is,

"Oh shit, I think I just met my mate."

Episode Sixteen: Not Looking

Foster

$\mathcal{W}$HAT IN THE actual fuck?!!! Of all the things I thought would happen today, finding my god damn mate was not one of them. I don't want a mate, and I never have. The only thing a mate can do for you is fuck with your god damn head, break your heart and destroy your life. Hell, just ask my mom. Oh wait, you can't; she died from her broken heart because of a useless mate. A pointless, good-for-nothing bond I neither wanted nor asked for.

"Hey Foss, you just missed the new girl Seamus hired." A low groan escapes me just as my wolf perks up. I pray to the moon Goddess he is not talking about the girl who just left. Looking up at the ceiling, I quietly ask whoever is listening to give me a damn break. When Hyde opens his mouth again, he dashes every prayer I throw out there. "You may have seen her. She left right before you came in."

Claim our mate, my wolf repeatedly growls in my head.

Shut up, furball, we aren't claiming shit; I snap back at him. Upon hearing me call him furball, his growls grow louder. He hates the nickname I gave him not long after I gained access to him when he kept pushing me to release him while I was coming to terms with having something else living inside my head.

"Her name is Shay...." This is the last thing I hear of Hyde's ongoing monolog. I am currently trying to shut my wolf the hell up.

Shay, her name just rolls off the tongue.

NO.

Shay. Shay. Shay. SSSHHHAAAYY. It's like a mantra. A mantra of what I plan on repeating as I claim what the moon Goddess has granted us.

Shut up, asshole. We are not; let me make this perfectly clear: NOT looking for a mate.

Speaking of tongues, I can't wait to run ours over her entire body.

I am going to shove you so far down that you will not see the light of day for a long damn time.

And did you smell her? God damn, she smelled like heaven. Let's go claim her. Like right now.

NO!

Yes.

NO! Absolutely fucking not.

Oh, I plan on doing lots, and let me make this clear LOTS of fucking where she's concerned.

You are not listening.

Nope, I'm definitely not listening, but I am thinking we might want to break your dry spell and use that limb dangling between your legs.

What the hell is your issue? You've never been this big of a pain in my ass before. I hiss at him.

Do you realize how long it's been? No? Well, neither can I. Our mate is here if you lift your nose and inhale enough. He forces my head up while making me breathe in the air around us. *Yep, her scent is still here, and she smells better than anything we have ever smelled before today.*

I don't care.

I do because blue balls are a thing, and ours are zooming past blue to an ugly fucking shade of purple.

"Foss? You okay?" This time it's not Hyde asking; it's Finch, and what I want to say is fuck no, I'm not okay, but I can't say this here.

"Hey, I need to go out for a run," I tell him quietly as I turn to walk towards the door.

"Hang on man. I'll come with you."

"No. You don't have to—"

"I know I don't have to do shit. I want to come." I can't really argue with him without telling him what has me so rattled. Nodding my head, I turn to go release my wolf; maybe if I let him out to run some of this pent-up energy off, he will back down about this whole mate issue. I am happy we don't know where this girl lives because I know nothing would stop him from trying to claim her.

"You want to head back to our pack lands?" Finch asks.

I take a quick look around the woods that butt up to the back of Stooges and will eventually lead us back to our pack. My final deciding factor is when my damn wolf practically slams against my mental walls trying to break free, "No. Here. Now." It is the only response I manage before I rush into the woods to strip my clothes before I drop into my wolf.

The instant I release him, he throws his head up, inhaling the surrounding air. I knew he was hoping to pick up her scent so he could follow her home. Fortunately, the wind has picked up enough to carry any lingering aroma of this girl away.

This girl? This girl! My wolf growls before he continues. *Her name is Shay. Go ahead, say it; the word just rolls off our tongue.*

Shut up and run, or this outing is over. I snap back at him.

Two hours later, I have run him to the point of exhaustion. I force my wolf to shift back as we arrive on pack land. To say he is pissed I did this would be a definite understatement as his growls rumble through me. Finch, being Finch, remains in his wolf, romping around me for several minutes. I have no damn idea how he has so much energy. We just ran for the last two hours, and here he is rolling on his back like a new pup before he flips back onto his feet to jump around us. I know he wants to continue running, but for the first time since we ran into that girl, I finally got my wolf to simmer down, and I need to take a minute.

When Finch realizes I have no intention of continuing our run, he shifts so he can lean against the rock I am resting on.

"That was great." There is no way in hell he will let this go that easily.

"Now, do you mind telling me what brought about this impromptu run today? I thought you wanted to shoot some pool. Not that I mind since I really didn't want to have my ass handed to me like every other time." And there it is. I know I should just tell him what happened, yet I have no intention of doing this because I also know he will never let it go if I do. He's worse than a girl when it comes to the mate bond. So I do the only thing I can think of that may get me out of this situation. I lie.

"My wolf has been scratching at me all day to release him, and I finally just had enough of his bitching. I figured if I let him loose tonight, maybe he would let me shoot some pool in peace tomorrow."

"So does this mean my ass-kicking in a round of pool has only been delayed?"

Laughing, I slug his arm before confirming, "Precisely. Did you think I was going to give you two nights off?" The look he gives me confirms he knows that won't happen. "Come on, race you back to our clothes. If we hurry I might even buy you a beer. That is, if, and it's a big damn if, you can beat me. Hell, I'll even give you a head start."

Finch doesn't wait for me to say anything else; he instantly drops into his wolf form before he streaks away from me.

He has to know he doesn't stand a chance. As I begin counting, my wolf's amusement in our coming chase is apparent. Finch may have never-ending stamina, but I'm fast, extremely fast.

Even giving him a full-minute head start wasn't enough for him to beat me back. When he returns I am fully dressed and tossing stones in a tin can.

"I don't know why I even bother."

"Me either."

"You don't have to be a dick; no one likes a dick." I raise my eyebrow, waiting for him to catch up to what he just said. "Yeah, okay, so I guess some people like a dick, but not that kind of dick, dick."

"Come on, asshole, I'll buy you a beer."

"Wait, I thought the free beer was contingent on me winning. I clearly didn't win." He laughs as he pulls his shirt back on.

"Let's just say I owe you one." And I do owe him. Thanks to Finch coming with me tonight, my wolf had enough fun that he dropped the constant badgering for me to find my mate. Finch has a way of calming me down, reeling me in, and keeping my head on my shoulders. The least I owe my cousin is a beer.

"Shit, no one ever said I was a stupid man. I may need a shot too. You know to mend my wounded heart."

"Wounded heart?"

"Yeah, on account of you traipsing all over it just to prove how fast you are. Can't you give your favorite cousin a win just once?"

"Now, where would the fun be in that?"

"I don't know about you, but I happen to think it would be loads of fun."

Laughing, I clap his shoulder as I tell him, "Come on sore loser, let your favorite cousin buy you a drink."

"Dude, you're my only cousin."

"Even if you had a hundred others, I would still be your favorite," I tell him as I lead him into the bar.

Episode Seventeen: Proof

Brady

"MAGGIE, I NEED you to tell me what bus she got on. I promise I won't hurt her; however, I can't make that same promise if dad, my uncle, or even Travis finds her first."

"Brady, we were all so…. So terrible to Shay. She deserves a chance."

"And she could have had that chance if she would have just left without stealing the money."

"I'm not so sure she took it." Maggie's response was little more than a whisper.

"Why the hell would you say something like that?"

"It's just…."

"What?"

"I don't think…."

"Are you seriously trying to say it's just a coincidence the money came up missing at the same time Shay took off?"

"Shay told me—" Maggie's response is cut short when the door flies open as Travis comes sauntering in. Her expression changes and she refuses to make eye contact with him. The floor, the ceiling, my desk, and her hands which are folded on her lap but not him. Clearing her throat, she quietly says, "I should go."

"Maggie?"

"I can't help you, Brady, because I don't know. Sorry." After her declaration, she practically ran out of the room I claimed as my office here in the packhouse.

"What's her problem?" Travis snips.

"I have no idea." For now, I decide to keep the little bit of information she did reveal to myself. I need to get to the bottom of this. I have to think like an alpha, and if I have any hopes of being a fair and just one, then I need to listen, not just assume. I need to think before I leap and something about Maggie's demeanor and responses makes me find it hard to believe just their friendship alone would cause Maggie to outright lie to me.

"Any word on that little fucking traitor?"

"No, nothing yet."

"And she," he jerks his head in the direction Maggie just went, "doesn't know anything?"

I wonder why he's so interested in what Maggie might know, "Nope. She checked in the day everyone was out looking several times, and I just questioned her again."

"She didn't know anything? Anything at all?"

"I already said no, Travis."

"No need to get snippy."

"And there's no need for me to answer the same question twice. Why the hell are you so damn worried about it?"

"Seriously? This bitch just stole the money for our hospital, and you wonder why I'm so hell-bent on finding out where she is. What kind of asshole do you think I am?"

"One who never took so much interest in pack affairs before."

"Hey, with your Alpha ceremony looming, I need to get my head in the game since I'll be your Beta."

That's a bit presumptuous. I mean, yeah, I always figured Travis would be the one who would sit as my Beta, but I never actually announced shit. Yet I also have other friends, and Colton has qualities that Travis doesn't, like empathy for one. Yet even I have to admit that when it comes to a battle, I prefer Travis over Colton standing next to me. Although maybe having someone who thinks first would be the better option. Previously, the answer to this question seemed obvious since Travis appears to be the best choice. He is stronger and faster than Colton, but if I plan on taking this pack in a new direction, is Travis or Colton the better option for my vision? These are all questions I will need to come up with answers for soon, just not today. Today I need to figure out this whole Shay issue. So instead of voicing any of these concerns, I simply nod my head in response to his statement.

Once again my door slams open before my dad and uncle storm in. Without knocking, I might add. What the actual hell? In what world do you just march into someone's office without being invited? Once I'm Alpha, shit is going to change around here.

"Is this how you find our missing money?"

"Is storming into my office your way?"

"Don't get cute, son. Because I do not find your sarcasm amusing."

"I plan on going into Whitefish today to show her picture around. I want to find out if anyone else saw her."

"What? You don't think she left in a truck like the guy at the store told Travis?"

"I don't think it hurts to ask again and maybe show her picture to some other people while we're there. Is that okay with you, oh magnanimous father, or shall I follow you and the other scouts around hoping to pick up a trail that is a week old?" My dad's Beta Owen snarls about the last part of my comment, but he doesn't say anything. I guess he figures that if dad isn't going to bitch about it, neither should he.

I had intended to go by myself; unfortunately, my dad's only directive was for me to take my future Beta Travis with me. So he believes the same thing Travis does, and as I said, I'm not sure who I will select, yet this is a conversation for another day. I plan to talk it over with my dad when I need to make my selection. It can't hurt to get his advice on the issue; even though I don't always agree with everything he does and says, I am smart enough to know I still have a lot to learn. I will listen to why he thinks Travis would make the best option.

Once in Whitefish, I began showing the only picture I could find of Shay to the different residents. It just goes to show how little our pack thought of her; the only photo is from over five years ago, and it's a fuzzy shot of Shay in the background.

Entering the store, Travis lifts his chin toward the only guy in the place. I take this to mean he is the one who told Travis and our scouts Shay left via truck heading East.

"Good afternoon, sir. My name is Brady."

"Howdy. How can I help you today, son?"

"I was hoping you could help me find my friend," I say as I hand him the picture. He takes one look at it before he looks past me toward Travis.

Shaking his head, he hands it back to me before advising, "No, not since she was here a week ago."

"Are you certain this is the girl who was in here that day?"

"I'll tell you the same thin' I told your other friend over there; she got in a truck headin' east. I haven't seen her or the money since then."

A phone call from my dad has me stepping outside to have some privacy. Well, as much as I can get standing on the side of a building. I figured Travis would follow me, but he seemed engrossed by something he found within the store.

"Did you discover anything?"

"Not yet, but I was in speaking with the clerk at the general store when you called. He is standing by his story about Shay leaving with a trucker heading east."

"Do you believe him?"

"Not sure yet. I want to talk with him a bit longer."

"If you think he's lying, make sure you get him talking."

"If he doesn't want to tell me—"

"Then you make him tell you by any means necessary. I'm sick of listening to your mother about this issue. It's time we find that girl and put an end to this shit."

I know there is no point in arguing with him. This would be an example of one of those things we don't agree on concerning the best way to deal with a difficult situation. I plan on handling things vastly different from my dad when, or should I say, if I become Alpha. I know my mom is harping on him day and night. She had it out for Shay before she left, and now that she's gone with the money, mom is damn near

110

murderous. After finishing my conversation, I go back into the store to collect Travis. I want to stop at the small diner, and if I can get away from Travis for a minute, I want to check at the bus station. When I walk inside, I find Travis grasping the guy's shirt tight in his fist as he is snarling something low.

I am instantly pissed when I realize he is doing precisely what my dad instructed me to do. Travis has not heard me come in for some unknown reason, and the store clerk has his full attention on the angry shifter before him. The entire interaction infuriates me. I also want answers, just not like this, making me snarl, "What the hell is going on?"

Travis remains unmoving, his gaze focused on the poor guy in front of him. Ordinarily, this would be enough to have most men squirming. Not this guy, though; for some reason, he stands his ground and refuses to back down.

"I think this asshole knows more than he is telling us."

"You need to back off, Travis."

"Not until he tells me what I need to know." Now that's an interesting choice of words he used, so I call him out.

"*You* need to know, or did you mean *we* need to know?"

"I meant we; this asshole is just frustrating the hell out of me." He yanks the guy closer as he growls. "Tell us the goddamn truth, old man."

"Let him go, Travis. Don't make me tell you again."

"Your dad said by any means necessary." Now how does he know that since his ass was in here when I had that conversation with dad? Apparently, my dad and one of my best friends have been talking without me. Well, I could give a shit less; if I have any hopes of being an Alpha, then I need to demand the respect you give to one now.

"Let. Him. Go. Right. Fucking. Now, Travis."

Episode Eighteen: Breaking Out

Shay

I CAN'T BELIEVE I just met my mate, and he walked away like I didn't exist. Maybe I'm wrong. Perhaps he isn't my mate. I mean, hell, it wouldn't be the first time I have been wrong about something. Besides, it's not like I am looking for or even want a mate. I just got away from a pack who ruled over me; the last thing I need to do is let some damn man take over their old role. I have had enough of living under someone else's thumb to last me a lifetime.

So that's it. I've made my decision; even if the moon Goddess deemed him to be my other half, I will just ignore the bond. He didn't seem to have any issues doing the same thing, so I shouldn't either. Who cares if he just so happens to be the most handsome man I have ever seen with deep, soulful amber eyes with flecks of gold. Yeah, this should be a piece of fucking cake. Here's hoping he was only passing through town and he's not a regular. If he does live in town, fingers crossed, he doesn't frequent Stooges.

Regardless sitting around worrying about it isn't going to help me, not to mention it is a beautiful night, and I haven't shifted in a while, leaving my wolf feeling anxious. Thank Goddess, she understands the circumstance we find ourselves in, so she hasn't pushed the issue much until seeing our mate tonight. She knows I have no intention of claiming him, and even though it goes against every piece of her soul, I believe she realizes why I am making this choice. A decision not just for me but for her as well. I will never again let anyone tell me my wolf does not need to be released, nor will I let anyone cage her ever again.

Adela used to do this as a punishment if she discovered I let my wolf out. She wanted my wolf to wither away much as Nan's has done. She would collar me so I could not release my wolf; this was the worst kind of torture. I could hear her whimpered cries in my head the entire time, almost as if the collar caused her physical pain. My heart broke every time she would howl out. Imagine having half of yourself removed, imprisoned, and you could feel their torment the entire time. This is what it is like to be collared. It only took one time, two excruciating months, for me to ensure no one ever saw me release my wolf again. I had to protect her from ever knowing that pain again.

Yet I think tonight she deserves to stretch her legs, feel the wind flowing through her fur, the moon's rays shining off her coat, and be free like I am now. Shortly after arriving in Lake, I found a second-hand store allowing me to purchase some other clothes. One of the things I bought was a dress; knowing this would let me easily slip it off and hide it so I could shift.

Ten minutes later I've hiked far enough into the woods to shed the dress and release my wolf.

Thank you, Shay. I hear her whisper through me. I know she has missed her morning runs, and now that I have found a relatively safe place to release her, I need to start doing it more often. I don't have to respond; she feels how much I have missed letting her do this, and she knows I love her. And even though I start my first job tomorrow, tonight is all about her; consequently, I will let her run for as long as she needs to.

She romps through the woods, playfully chasing other animals, rolling on the ground, splashing through the stream, and generally just acting like she is a new pup. It's not until she lies on an outcrop of rocks at the edge of the stream, completely at peace for the first time ever, that I feel my heart tighten, knowing she has never been able to do this before tonight. Suddenly I realized it was not just me held within the prison of our previous pack; it was both of us, and knowing I allowed this to happen to her hurts me more than anything Tobias and Adela did to me.

Don't feel sad, Shay.

I'm sorry I should have left a long time ago, I quietly confess.

You never knew any other existence. I'm proud of you.

You shouldn't be. You should hate me for keeping you imprisoned for so long.

When you found the strength to leave, you did. You did it without knowing how we would survive and without any help from anyone else, fully knowing we could never return. You should be proud of yourself too.

I know she is trying to absolve me of any responsibility for how she has had to live. As I quietly reflect on our life thus far, she lays her head on her paws and drifts off to sleep. I have no

114

idea how long we slept under the starry sky since I also dozed off. It's not until I feel her shaking off the loose debris clinging to her fur that I am roused awake.

Thank you for allowing me this time, but you need to rest in a warm bed. This is when I realize how cold the air has become. My wolf expertly navigates the terrain leading us back to where I hid the dress. After shifting back and sliding the dress over my head, I make my way toward our hotel. Halfway across an abandoned lot, something in our surroundings has my wolf snapping to high alert as a low growl rumbles through me.

Hide, Shay. She keeps repeating. She has never steered me wrong before, so I am not about to start ignoring her now. I rush inside a shed just before headlights flood the area I was just standing in. Ducking down as low as I can behind a table, it's not until the headlights shut off that I realize who's out there. Thanks to my wolf's keen senses, I did not have to come face-to-face with him. It's the asshole I ran into the first night I was at Stooges. The thought of his hands on me makes my skin crawl. Further driving home, this guy and Travis are one and the same.

Another car pulls in. This time the person does not turn out their headlights, so I cannot identify who is in the car. The asshole gets out of his car before climbing into the other vehicle's passenger side. Figuring when he opens the door, the overhead light will come on, illuminating whoever is in the new car; when this does not happen, I am left wondering who is in there. The asshole quietly closes the door, concealing the identity of whoever is in there from the outside world. I almost jump out of my skin when music booms through the air. I realize this is to drown out their conversation since even with my wolf's acute hearing, I can only make out a few words of what they are saying.

Some of these words include tired, fight, money, no gun, etcetera, but one word causes the hairs on my arm to stand up; this word is dead. Oh my god, are they talking about killing someone? Straining my ears, I try to pick up any other part of their conversation; a name would be great. Even if I don't know the person, maybe Hyde or Seamus will; if they do, I can call this in anonymously.

Taking a dangerous risk, I slip out from behind the table and scamper over to some barrels. From my new vantage point, I still can't hear much, but now the glare from the headlights has been cut down, I can see the silhouette of the other person. He is an extremely large man, but other than that, I cannot make out any other features. When the passenger door suddenly whips open, I damn near fall on my ass trying to duck further behind the barrels. My foot slips across the gravel, a sound the asshole must have heard since he turns to inspect the shed.

Shit—shit—shit, if he comes over here, I will have no choice other than shift to get away from him. I can only pray he doesn't have a gun because as fast as my wolf is, she cannot outrun a bullet.

"Is there a problem?" This is the first time I hear the newcomer's muffled voice.

Asshole cranes his head, "Not sure." He slowly begins creeping towards the shed I am using as my hideout. Damn it to hell; why didn't I just stay behind the damn table? These barrels don't offer anywhere near as much cover as it did. My heart almost drops to my feet when I hear him cock a gun, placing a bullet in the chamber. There is no way he'd miss me at this range if I shifted now. Closing my eyes, I will my breathing to slow down. The next thing that happens is both a godsend and the worst thing I have ever endured when a cat scampers past me. The blast from the gun he is holding is deafening in this confined space, but the howls of pain from the poor cat make this situation heartbreaking.

"Not anymore." His cold response makes me furious. He just shot this poor animal for no reason, and now, on top of it, he doesn't even have the decency to end its suffering. With this one act, he just soared past Travis in the asshole department, landing purely in the monster zone.

Episode Nineteen: First

Shay

*B*Y THE TIME they left, the cat had stopped crying, and once I crept out from my hiding spot, he was gone. I feel awful because I know this poor thing just saved my life as much as I know my actions ended his. The elation I felt earlier, having released my wolf, is gone as I slowly shuffle back to the hotel. As much as I disliked this guy the first time I bumped into him, I believe I can now say I have soared past dislike and landed squarely on loathe; I loathe this man. How anyone can be so heartless as to leave an animal to suffer is beyond me.

Climbing into bed, I try to concentrate on the joy my wolf experienced tonight and not the disturbing events from my journey home. But I am finding it difficult not to let my mind wander to who they could have been talking about. Not to mention the clandestine conversation... Was it really about killing someone? After tossing and turning for several hours, I finally managed to drift off to a night of restless, nightmare-filled sleep.

For the first time since my parents died, I sleep past six o'clock in the morning. When I finally peel my eyes open, I realize that too much light is coming through the window. A quick glance at the clock reveals it is almost nine o'clock.

"Shit!" I shout as I throw the blankets back. Although I have no idea why I am so damn worried about it, it's not like I am going to be late for work. Seamus told me I didn't need to be there until five o'clock. I figured I could use the time between now and when I have to be at work to look for somewhere else to live. After a brief shower, I walk several blocks to a small, locally owned convenience store.

During this trip I met two more of my neighbors, a sweet elderly couple who runs the shop. They helped me find everything I needed and refused to let me pay for half of the items I purchased. They tried to give me everything for free, but I declined, telling them I liked their little store and would prefer for it to remain open, which would only happen if they stopped giving away their merchandise for free.

Sitting on the bed with my legs crossed, eating a snack bag of chips, I peruse the available rental properties listed in the local newspaper. I'm sure it comes as no surprise the options were scanty at best. The possibility of me being homeless is becoming less possibility and moving closer to my new reality. Here's hoping any tips I get tonight will help me keep this room.

By four o'clock, I am already gathering my stuff to go to work. I know there will come a day when I will ring out every possible second of my time before I have to be there, but with today being my first day, not to mention my first day at my first job ever, I am ready to go in now. I can sit here clock-watching until 4:45 when I would have to leave, so I'm on time, or I can just end my torment and go now. Now wins out.

As I place my hand on the doorknob, I cannot help but feel my nerves are worse than at any other time today. Taking a second to try to calm myself, I silently pray for a nice quiet night, at least until I figure out what I'm doing.

Walking into the bar, I wonder if exploding hearts are actually a thing because if mine beats any more frantically, I may find out.

"Shay," Hyde yells his greeting like the gang at Cheers (it's one of the few shows I was permitted to watch on occasion back at the packhouse) would yell Norm. I can't help chuckling as I imagine myself dressed like Norm while Hyde is dressed like Cliff and the image of Seamus about has me laughing out loud. Is there any doubt about who he'd be dressed up like? Carla, of course.

Plopping next to him on the stool, "Hey."

"You ready for tonight?"

"Oh god, what's tonight?" I ask as a whole new panic begins to surface. What if Seamus had me start today because they have some big event planned or party; please don't let it be a party. I really don't want to screw up something on someone's big day, whatever that big day may be. Wiping my sweaty palms on my jeans, I hope my utter terror is not displayed on my face right now.

"Tuesday." This time I know my face showcases my turbulent emotions because he laughs before clarifying. "Don't sweat it, kiddo. Tuesdays are normally pretty tame around here."

"So, no big event?"

"Nope, not that I know of."

"No party?"

"I don't think so; hey Jerry, is there a party here tonight?"

"Party? I wanna party," he slurs before finishing with his typical response, a hiccup.

"See, no party," Hyde advises as he shrugs his shoulders.

"Ummm, are you sure he's the best person to ask?"

"Trust me, if there was a party here, he'd know about it."

"Okay, I guess I'll take your word for it," I say while trying to calm my nerves. Hyde, on the other hand, grins before giving me a little wink.

"Hey, you ol' codger, get your arse out here," Hyde yells towards the kitchen.

"Houl yer whisht! Yer acting the maggot." Seamus bellows from the kitchen, resulting in a roaring laugh from Hyde in response. His amusement is infectious, and I can't help the little giggle escaping me.

"Okay, I've gotta admit I have no idea what he just said."

"He told me to shut up, then informed me I'm acting like a jerk."

"And these are real sayings?"

"In Ireland, yeah. Just a shame the ol' codger hasn't figured out we're in AMERICA," Hyde playfully shouts the last part with a beaming grin.

"Bullocks!" Seamus grumbles as he comes through the swinging door that separates the kitchen area from the bar. When Seamus sees me sitting here, he grins, realizing why Hyde is giving him such a hard time. "How ya?"

I look from Seamus to Hyde before he tells me, "He wants to know how you're doing."

"Oh, I'm good, although I admit I'm a little nervous."

"Ah, I'll get ya a wee half'n' that'll help."

"No, it's probably best if I don't start drinking now," I tell him placing my hand on his arm before he can walk away.

"Aye, suit yer self. You ready?"

Taking a deep breath, I stand up enthusiastically, declaring, "Absolutely."

That a girl, Shay. My wolf praises.

Since I came in early, the girl who is supposed to show me the ropes isn't here yet, so Seamus shows me around the bar. He gets me the keys to the stock room and tells me he'll get me a key made for the door. The thought of having to learn how to use the cash register scared the shit out of me for some unknown reason, but it is actually a lot easier to operate than I thought it would be.; the only thing I am more scared of is having to learn all the drinks I've never heard of.

Currently, there are only a handful of customers scattered around here. Most are sitting at the bar, a couple, if the googly eyes they keep giving one another is anything to go by, is seated at a table, and then four guys are playing darts. We had a dart board at the packhouse, and I would play when no one was around. I actually got pretty good at it. Maybe if Seamus doesn't mind the next time I'm off, I can come in and play a round. While I like playing 301 and around the clock, cricket is hands down my favorite. I tend to rack up points on bullseye since this is what I practice hitting the most. I normally run up two hundred points on bullseye alone within my first seven to ten throws. I have never actually gotten to play against anyone, even though I always wanted to see how I would do. Perhaps I can persuade Hyde to play a game or two.

Seamus told me I could stick with grabbing beers; he and Mandy would handle the mixed drinks tonight, and I could waitress if the bar gets busy enough. While he shows me where the beers are in each cooler, a customer places his beer on the counter's edge. Without taking my eyes off Seamus, I grab a beer from the cooler, open it, set it in front of the guy, and accept the money.

"Aye, I think yer gonna fit in just fine," Seamus tells me with a grin.

The only thing I can think of is I sure hope so.

Episode Twenty: Move It, Move It

Shay

*A*ROUND FIVE O'CLOCK more people filter in, which makes sense since it is a weekday and the majority of people work during the week, not to mention most people work until five or six. All the previously empty stools at the bar are now filled, and several of the tables are. At half-past the hour, I notice Seamus keeps glancing at the clock mumbling something under his breath. After he does this three times, I realize the girl who was supposed to be my trainer hasn't arrived yet. I don't know her or if she is normally late, but if the color of Seamus's face is anything to go by, he looks like he is about to blow his top. I don't think I have ever witnessed this shade of red before.

Ten minutes later, the door flies open with a woman about my age running through it.

"Shit Seamus, I'm sorry my flight got in late last night, and I overslept."

"Bollocks." He quickly responds before grumbling, "Mandy, Shay. Shay, Mandy." This is all the introduction we get.

Walking towards her so I could formally introduce myself, I wait until she is done tying her hair back before sticking my hand out. She graciously accepts and tells me with a beaming smile, "Nice to have you with us."

"Thanks."

"I've been out of town for a few days. When did you start?"

Returning her smile with a grin of my own, I respond, "Today."

"No shit, well welcome to the family. So let me make some introductions. This handsome gentleman is Hyde."

"We're old friends," I say, looking over at him. I can't tell if the grin covering his face is because he's being friendly or if it's because I called him a friend. Either way, it increases mine as I tell her, "He actually helped me get the job."

"Well, good on ya, Hyde. If you know Hyde, I am going to assume you know our bar mascot then too?"

"Jerry? Yeah, we've met as well." Jerry looks up. With his typical wave, he wiggles just his fingers, and this time I can't help but return the gesture.

"Do you know anyone else?"

"Besides Seamus. No. Not really."

She takes me around to each of the customers to make the introductions before warning them all to be nice to me. Something tells me this won't be an issue. I can't imagine any of these people being mean to anyone. Well, except for the asshole, something tells me he is nothing but trouble, yet I also believe Seamus's rules are the law here at the bar. Since he is the size of a small barn, I can't imagine many people would want him purposely pissed at them.

By six o'clock, the bar is standing room only. I admit I'm shocked at how busy it is on a weekday.

"Wow, is this place always this busy?" I ask Mandy.

"Every Tuesday and the weekends, absolutely."

"What's so special about Tuesday?"

"Oh, we host either dart or pool tournaments every Tuesday."

Upon hearing this, I look over at Hyde, narrowing my eyes at him. On the other hand, he smiles, showing too many teeth before responding, "Oh, did I forget to mention that?"

Nodding my head with my eyes wide, I playfully respond, "Why yes—yes, you did."

"My bad." Now it is not just his lips pulled back as far as he can get them, but his eyes are the size of saucers. "Do you happen to play either one of them?"

"Never played pool, but I have played darts. And don't change the subject; you and I are not done talking about this 'nothing is happening here tonight' thing. You're just lucky I have a couple of customers I need to attend to first, mister."

After this, I move farther down the bar to handle several people who have been patiently waiting for their drinks. A petite girl wraps her arms around Jerry.

"Hey, Jerry, how's your night going so far?"

"Peaches and," hiccup, "cream."

"Well, that sounds downright yummy."

"You have…. No…. no idea," he stutters. "Have you met my new friend?"

"I don't believe I've had the pleasure."

Hiccup, "This here's Shay. Shay, this is the sweet and lo," hiccup. Man trying to get through an entire conversation with Jerry must take a while. ".... vable. Lovable Nessie."

"Now, Jerry," she says slowly. Her tone is akin to how you would speak to a toddler. "we've talked about this several times. I am not the elusive monster living in Loch Ness over in Scotland." Moving her eyes up to me before offering her hand, she informs me, "It's just Ness. Well, actually, Vanessa, but I go by Ness."

"Nice to meet you, Ness," I reply, taking her hand in mine. She's a pretty girl, around five feet maybe two inches, with long chestnut-colored hair and Jade eyes. Her smile lights up her entire face, and my first impression is she doesn't have a mean bone in her body.

"You're new around here, aren't you?"

"Yep, just arrived."

"Why on earth would you choose Lake as the place you want to settle down in? Most folks around these parts are dying to get out."

"Not," hiccup, "me."

"Something tells me you're the exception to most things, Jerry," I joke.

"I am quite the ex.... Exception."

"Exceptional, Jerry." Ness smiles at him. "Do you have family around here, Shay?" As nice as she seems, I'm not ready to talk about myself with anyone. Maybe in the future, maybe never. Either way, this is not a conversation to have tonight.

"Nope, it's just me. So tell me about the tournament the bar hosts."

"Oh, it was Seamus's idea. Something for the locals to do to get them out of their houses. It can get kind of crazy here on

Tuesday because it's the place to be. Have you ever worked as a bartender before?"

"Nope, this is the first time, but Mandy has been great."

"Yeah, she's only here for," cue the.... Hiccup. "Foster."

"What's a Foster?"

"Not what, who. Foster is my cousin, and you know darn good and well, Jerry, that Foss will never entertain her."

"Regardless, that girl wants to climb him like a cat up a pole. Meow." When he swipes his fingers out like a cat's claw, both Ness and I can't help but laugh, which pleases Jerry to no end.

"It was nice meeting you, Shay. If you have a second, stop at my table so I can introduce you to my friends. As for you, Mr. Jokester, it will never happen. Foss is not like that, and you know it."

"Meow," he slurs. She shakes her head before heading back to her table, where several other young women are waiting. I don't miss how almost every single guy and some of the not-so-single men turn to watch her glide back towards her friends.

People continue filtering in for the next fifteen minutes. I'm told the tournament doesn't start until seven; this way, the guys who work at the mill can also participate in it. Seamus hands me a tray filled with a bunch of girly cocktails and points at Ness's table before mumbling to meet some people my age; it would be good for me. I never really saw the attraction to drinking something as sweet as many of these cocktails, but then again, I have never had one before either.

Carefully navigating through the crowd, I only have one almost mishap when a guy backs into me. He immediately began profusely apologizing to me until I assured him it was my fault. After he helps me steady the drinks, I start my slow trek to her table again. I can see the beaming smile as she watches me traverse the mob of patrons. Thankfully, I finally arrived at her table with only a few minor spills along the way.

"You made it." Ness grins at me.

"Yeah, barely," I chuckle. "I thought for sure I was going to dump the entire tray when the big guy backed into me."

"That's Denver; he has the grace of a bull but the heart of an elephant. Anyway, everyone, this is Shay. Shay, this is my best friend Lindsey, her cousin—"

"Hey," the cousin protested.

"And another one of my best friends, El. Better?" El grins at her. "Let's just say these are all my best friends that way no one gets their panties in a twist," Ness wrinkles her nose at El, who rolls her eyes at Ness. "This lovely lady is April, and sitting next to her is Sarah."

"It's nice to meet you." All the women sitting at the table give me a warm welcome. Each has their own set of questions about where I'm from, why I moved there, where my family is, and so on. I dodged their inquiries and managed to turn the focus back to them each time. Hell, I impressed myself with how expertly I handled the situation. Score one for Shay. I admit to doing a happy dance in my head until Ness ends by saying,

"Oh, and this is my brother Finch and cousin Foster. Guys, this is Shay." When I turn, my heart drops to my feet when I discover my mate standing there. Well, there goes the only friend I've made in this town aside from Hyde. I guess I'm just not meant to have friends. Right? Right.

Episode Twenty-One: And Go

Shay

I MANAGE TO mumble a quick hello, yet little else since my throat could currently be compared to the Mojave; while he doesn't say anything, to be honest, he doesn't even look at me. I return behind the bar so I can put as much space as possible between me and my.... Well, you know what he is; we don't need to keep rehashing that shit.

Did you smell how wonderful his scent is? My wolf practically purrs.

Hey, you're a badass wolf, not a meek kitty cat. There will be absolutely no damn purring, and no, I did not smell him. I snap back.

Now, Shay, you know you can't lie to me. I live inside you until you release me. I feel what you feel, I hear what you hear, I smell what—

Yeah-yeah, I get it. Now be quiet. Thankfully she quiets down after this, but I can feel the pull she has to his wolf, which tells me what side of the fence she is leaning towards on the whole not wanting a mate thing.

The bar is so busy tonight it leaves me very little time to admire the muscular tone physique of a certain someone. Where Brady has a lean athletic body from sparring with the other wolves in the pack, this guy's body comes from a lot of hard physical work. I also happen to catch the way his shirt rides up just enough to reveal his well-scalped abs each time he raises his arm, not to mention how the light catches the gold in his eyes when he laughs. Yeah, I'm not watching him at all. Fortunately, he never once looks in my direction, further confirming that he doesn't know, doesn't care, or doesn't want me as his mate.

I wonder if his wolf has the same dark hair.

Well, we are not going to find out, so simmer down. I chastise my wolf when if I am being honest, I should be reprimanding myself, not her. Mandy's groans as she readjusted her breast has me looking over towards her, and unlike my occasional glances, she is staring at him like he is the last drink of water on earth.

"Hmmm—hmmm."

"You might as well give it up, Mandy. He doesn't date any of the girls in town and absolutely none of the girls who work here."

"Give me five minutes, and I could change his mind." She replies in a sultry, mumbled voice. I can't help the grin I give her as I watch her lick her lips while Hyde merely shakes his head. Okay, note to self…. steer clear of him at all costs. We don't need another Natashia on our hands. While Mandy continues to admire the sights, I busy myself with filling drink orders, running from one customer to the next. I don't know if every

131

night is like this or if the customers are just giving the new girl a break since the only thing they ask for is beer or shots. I'm hoping this will not become a repeat of the kitchen back at the packhouse where I do all the work and Mandy stands around pretending she is busy. Especially since Hyde has been patiently waiting for a beer for several minutes. He is sitting at the other end of the bar, which she is supposed to be taking care of. At least this is how I assume it's supposed to work; she takes care of half the bar, I take care of the other half while Seamus....

"Pig's arse," he yells as something crashes to the floor.

.... takes care of the kitchen or as best as he can. I can't help but notice most customers are now coming strictly to my end of the bar to place their orders. Not Hyde though; he is patiently waiting. I mean, how bad would that look if Hyde got up and came down here just to get a beer since she's standing five feet away from him, twirling her hair. Goddess, give me strength. Deciding my friend has waited long enough, I rush down and grab his beer choice on my way. Twisting off the cap, I set it in front of him, causing him to mouth a silent "Thank you."

"Shay. Right?" I look up to find who I am going to say is Finch since Ness already told me Mandy has a thing for Foster, and her attention is not directed at the guy standing in front of me.

"Yeah, and your Finch."

"Nailed it, and can I say I'm happy you know who I am." He gives me a boyish grin. I'm willing to bet he is used to getting what he wants when he flashes this smile at anyone. I imagine not many females can resist it, not to mention some men as well. A hundred to one says he uses it to his advantage.

"Ness introduced you when you came in."

"Ah, but she never said which of us was Finch, and which of us is Foster. You figured that out all on your own. Were you asking about me?"

Returning his grin with one of my own, I lean across the bar, which has him mirroring the action until we are mere inches apart. All this so he can hear my quiet confession, "Yeah, I used my immense powers of deduction and figured out Mandy has a thing for Foster. Since her eyes are currently glued on the guy standing over by Ness, this must make you Finch."

"Ouch, you wound me. Here I thought you may be falling in love."

"Sorry big guy, now can I get you something?"

"I need to get another round for the girls and four draft beers for my buddies and me."

"Oh damn. Okay, I can figure this out. I'll make the shit out of those drinks." I confidently declare.

"I think they would prefer if you hold the shit," he tells me with a grin.

"Right. So no shit. I can do this." I look at all the bottles behind me, and for the first time tonight, I feel hopelessly overwhelmed when I realize I don't have the first clue what they are even drinking. Seamus made their first round, and Mandy made the second, making me look over at him before giving him a sheepish grin and asking, "Do you have any idea what Ness and her friends were drinking?"

"I think a peach daiquiri, or maybe it was a margarita? Hell, just give them something peach flavored, and they'll be happy as clams." I beg to differ because if it tastes like shit they may run me out of the bar. Seeing another opportunity to go over and talk to Foster, Mandy jumps in.

"You can get the beers for the guys. I'll make Ness and her friends their drinks and bring them over."

"I bet you will," Finch and Hyde say simultaneously before high-fiving each other. Gathering the beers, I hand them to Finch just as the big guy named Denver comes over grumbling.

"Seamus." This guy yells a little louder when he doesn't answer. "Seamus, get your ass out here."

"Houl yer whisht, you damn muppet." Hey, I know what this means. Progress. Yay me.

"We need you."

"What are you on about?"

"We're a player short for the tourney. Come on."

"Not a twitter of wit. Are you pissed as a fart?" And we're back to no clue what my boss just said.

"Speak English, you daft fucker."

"That was English, you egit. Can't ya see I'm busy?"

"Oh, I'll do it," Mandy jumps forward quickly.

"No offense, Man, but you can't hit the broad side of a barn with a semi," Hyde tells her as he pats her shoulder.

"So they just need another body. I can be that body," she announces before further mumbling, "especially if the body is for Foster."

"I have an idea." Everyone turns to look at Hyde. "Why doesn't Shay do it?" he suggests, which results in my eyes widening while my mouth gapes open.

Slamming my mouth shut, I am quick to decline, "I couldn't possibly…. I'm working, and with it being my first night and all—"

"Nonsense. Isn't that right, Seamus," Hyde interrupts. I am so going to smack the shit out of him.

"Can you throw darts?" Seamus asks.

"Can she throw darts…. I'll have you all know my money's on Shay tonight." I suddenly regret having told him I know how to play darts. Why, oh why, couldn't tonight be a pool tournament?

"I only said I know-how. I never said I'm any good at it," I retort, looking directly at Hyde while shaking my head slightly. I hope this asshole—and I use asshole in the "I love this guy, but I am so going to kill him if he opens his mouth again" kind of way—will shut up.

For the first time since this Denver guy barreled up here bellowing for Seamus, I notice the entire bar seems to be enthralled by our conversation. Seeing all their gazes directed at me makes my already red face turn an even brighter shade of crimson.

Damn it to hell. The only thing I wanted to do was come in, do my job, and go home. I have no desire to see my mate, who doesn't want anything to do with me, which is fine since I am on the same ship. I didn't want to have the entire bar staring at me either, and I certainly didn't plan on playing darts in front of a room full of people I had only just met tonight. My anxiety is getting the better of me, and as a result, my hands are now sweating buckets. Wiping them down the front of my jeans, I look back over at Hyde with what I hope is an expression of *help get me out of this damn situation you put me in.*

But does he help me? No! No, he does not; instead, he freaking winks before yelling, "I've got twenty on the new girl."

"I am so going to kick your ass," I mutter so only Hyde can hear me as I stalk by.

"You can thank me later," he laughs.

"Well, get yer arse over there and represent me bar," Seamus tells me with a sly grin.

Episode Twenty-Two: Tourney

Foster

MY WOLF PERKS up the second we enter the bar since her scent hangs heavy in the air. It would be impossible to miss since she smells like the honeysuckle surrounding my cabin after it rains. Great, now I'm going to think about her every time I see it.

Or smell it, my wolf declares. I don't know if he thinks he is helping; I can assure you he is not.

I can solve that issue; I'll simply cut it down, I retort.

And take away that delicious fragrance. My money's on no. He is really starting to piss me off.

You don't have any money, asshole.

Of course, I do.

Where? My response comes out just as skeptical as I am feeling.

Your bank account.

So we're talking about My money.

No, we're talking about Our money.

Glancing around the bar, I discover her standing at the table Ness is occupying. Ness, her friends, and the new girl all seem to be having a grand time chatting it up with one another, and is that a god damn tray in her hand? For fuck's sake, please tell me Seamus didn't hire this girl to work here. Of all the damn girls he could hire, she has to be the one he picks. Her long blonde hair gleams under the lights from the bar, and I can't help but follow her hand as she pushes an unruly lock of her mane behind her ear for the second time.

Claim mate, my wolf tells me excitedly.

You shut up, or we can leave right fuckin now, I growl at him. This seems to do the trick because he goes silent, at least for the time being.

"You coming, Foss, or what?" Finch yells as he motions for me to follow him to the table. I wonder if it's too late to just go home. Damn it, I can't keep running every time she shows up, especially since it appears she now works at my favorite bar. It doesn't matter that Stooges is also the only bar in town because if there were other options, I would still rather spend my time here than at any other watering hole. I like Seamus. He's a damn fine man who knows all about the pack of shifters living just outside of town, yet he has never revealed our secret to anyone.

Deciding the best way to move past whatever the initial interest my wolf has in her is to immerse myself in my normal routine, which includes playing pool or darts. To hell with it; I am definitely participating in the tournament tonight. Walking up, I hear my cousin introduce us, and when she turns to look at Finch and me, I can't help but become lost in the sea of blue looking back at me. Shit, but she has the bluest eyes I have ever

137

seen. This weakens my resolve for a split second, but I quickly remind myself why I don't want a damn mate. With this firmly rooted in mind ignoring the new bartender has become significantly easier.

The good news is that she seems to be on the same page as I am, or she hasn't realized we're mates yet, which I find highly doubtful. Thankfully she doesn't stick around, which eliminates any awkward conversation.

Good thing? You think this is a good thing? This is a god damn tragedy. If our mate rejects us, we may never find anyone ever again. My wolf's angry growls have a smirk crossing my face.

Are you listening to me, asshole?

Nope.

"Hey Foss, you ready to get your ass kicked?" Denver asks me.

"Is someone who can actually throw darts coming tonight?"

"No, jackass, I'm going to kick your ass. Me. No one else needed."

"I'll take some of that action," Atlas announces as he drinks the rest of the beer. The grin covering Denver's face upon hearing Atlas's confidence fades just as fast when he finishes, "On Foster, of course."

"Hey."

"Sorry brother, now if you all want to arm wrestle hands down, you get my vote for the win."

Denver raises his eyebrow, waiting to see if I will take up the challenge. Not being one to shy away from anything, part of me wants to clear the table so we can settle this right now, but the more logical part of me knows this gargantuan asshole will have no problem taking me down. I'm still not saying it isn't a possibility in the future; I just need to practice before I take him on.

"Anything is possible." I grin while clapping his back.

"That's not a no." We all laugh when he flexes his arm.

"Hey, Fincher, I'll buy if you go up and grab us a round," Atlas tells him.

"Ooh, one for us too?" Ness bats her eyelashes at him. Very few men can resist her feminine wiles, Atlas and Denver included. She always bitched about her girlfriends crushing on Finch and me when we were growing up, but we had to warn our friends to stay away from her. Hell, I even had to threaten my best friend when I found Archer's gaze lingering just a bit too long for my liking.

"And a drink for the table of beautiful women." Ness squeals, clapping her hands while the remaining women gush over him calling them beautiful.

The loud shouts, accompanied by a crash from the kitchen, pull my attention towards the bar, and Shay floats across my field of vision. She's practically running from one customer to the next while the other barmaid, Mandy, seems to be busy watching me. The grin covering her face as Jerry jokes with her is quite the sight to behold.

See, you do like looking at her.

No, I appreciate hard work, furball.

Up yours, asshole, and you keep telling yourself that. Maybe someday you might actually convince yourself.

"We don't have enough people who want to participate in the tournament tonight." Ed comes over to inform us. He's the foreman at the mill and helps organize the event every Tuesday. I'm not sure we would still be doing this if not for him.

"Oh, hell no! I have been practicing all week, so I can take this asshole down. We are having that damn tournament tonight."

"Sorry, Denver, but we're one person short, and no one wants to drop out."

"I'll take care of it. Don't cancel shit," Denver mutters as he storms up to the bar. I don't know why he wants to challenge me so damn bad; he has never beaten me, never even come close. Most of the time, we end up in different brackets, and he gets knocked out before he ever gets the chance. I knew who he was going to get. Seamus has filled in several times when this has happened in the past. And sure enough, he begins bellowing Seamus's name before he is fully up to the bar. Denver better cool his jets if he wants the Irish man to compete.

As suspected, Seamus isn't pleased with Denver's approach and flat-out tells him to piss off.

"Foster." When I turn, I find Ness beckoning me over to her table. I don't miss Lindsey's face turning red as her eyes drop to her empty drink. Something tells me this request may directly correlate with whatever the hell has her turning this shade.

"Ness." Trying not to embarrass Lindsey further, I keep my focus on my cousin.

"Linds wants to learn how to throw darts. Do you think maybe next time you and Finch come here, we could meet you so you could teach both of us how to play?" I begin to say no, but I have never been able to deny her anything, especially when she gives me those damn sad puppy dog eyes she is currently flashing at me.

"I guess."

"Yay." Somewhere behind me, I hear someone saying something about the new girl. I don't have to worry about her

140

playing darts; there is no way in hell Seamus would pay her to play in the tournament. It isn't until Ness speaks again that I realize how wrong I am....

"Oh, I guess Shay is going to step in and play since Seamus can't." No damn way! Nessie has to be mistaken.

"I've got twenty on the new girl," and just like that, I know there is a damn way, and it seems Hyde is the one behind it. I'll have to remember to thank him next time we're alone.

Episode Twenty-Three: Just Throw It

Shay

I AM TOTALLY going to throw this so I can return to work. Plus, I must admit I will feel vindicated since Hyde will lose the money he just bet on me. I realize no one knows why I would oppose doing this. Well, that is except for him. He probably would understand not wanting to be in the same space as me; hell, he doesn't seem to like me in the same state, let alone the same dart tournament he's participating in. Oh. My. Goddess. What if he thinks I volunteered to play darts to be close to him? Yeah, I totally need to throw this. Just throw it and get my ass back behind the bar where it belongs. That is until I hear Seamus's directive.

"Well, get yer arse over there and represent me bar." Shit. I can't let him down, not when he has been so kind to me since showing up here in Lake. I can't just throw it. My only saving grace is I haven't actually ever played against anyone, so maybe it won't be as easy as playing by yourself. After all, there is no pressure when it is just you against you.

"So, are you the one who is saving the dart tournament from being canceled?" a man asks me as I approach. He has a pleasant face with bright, sparkling eyes. Gray peppers his brown hair, but it is his friendly smile that instantly puts me at ease.

"Guess I am."

"Fantastic. What's your name?"

"Shay."

"Well, it's a pleasure to meet you, Shay. My name is Ed. If you have any questions, just let me know."

"Ah, what am I supposed to do?"

"Have you taken part in a dart tournament before?" When I shake my head, he grabs the bill of his ball cap and begins scratching the hat back and forth on his head.

"A pool tournament then?" Again I confess I have not. I can feel my face beginning to heat up as I realize everyone is now staring at me. If I could fall into a deep dark pit to hell, I think it may be preferential to having every set of eyes in this place sizing up the newbie. The thought of strangling Hyde for getting me into this situation pushes front and center in my mind, but it's only fleeting when I look over towards him only to find him giving me a thumbs up.

"So I take it you probably don't understand how the brackets work then either. Right?"

"I'm sorry. Maybe this was a bad idea." Without thinking, I glance over at Foster. I can't tell if the look of irritation has anything to do with me being a part of the tournament or if it's because I have no freaking clue what I'm doing, resulting in their competition being held up.

"Nonsense, we can figure it out and make sure you get to where you need to be," the smile he gave me when I first approached is back, and I have to admit it does have a way of putting me at ease even with the scowl being thrown at me from not only Foster but Mandy too. Great, just fan-fucking-tastic. I get away from one crazy girl to piss off another.

"No worries, Ed, I can help her." If that voice belongs to who I think it does, no damn way am I doing this. Turning slowly to confirm what I already know, my worst fears are realized when I find the asshole standing there grinning down at me.

"Great, thanks for helping out, Max," so the asshole has a name. Well, Max, you can just sod off. I don't want nor do I need your freaking help. I can read; I'll just figure this out on my own since I have no desire to have you anywhere near me. These are all things I want to shout, but the staring eyes of everyone else in the room silence any objection. Goddess, why do you hate me so much?

Just throw it, Shay. You can explain to Seamus why later. I'm sure if you tell him this guy makes you feel uneasy, he'd understand.

Uneasy doesn't cover it. This guy gives me the creeps.

Max's hand on my lower back causes a chill to move up my spine as he guides me toward the dartboard I am slated to play on. The thought of this slimy bastard touching me even through my clothes makes me want to burn them and scour the spot where his hand is resting with hot, and I mean scalding hot, water.

"This is Shelly. Shelly, it is my extreme pleasure to introduce you to—" His eyes roam over my frame, but I realize asshole (yeah, even though I know his name is Max, asshole just seems to fit him better) doesn't know my name.

"Oh right, I'm Shay," I say, directing my attention at the woman who will be my first opponent, fully ignoring the asshole at my back.

"Alright, everyone, you know the rules. Keep it clean, no fighting, and may the best man," he turns, bowing towards Shelly and me before continuing, "or woman, win. But just so you all know, my money is on one of these two taking it all." He winks towards us before Shelly indicates I should go ahead and begin.

Walking up, I choose the darts I plan on using for the tournament's duration. The weight feels good, the flights are not bent, and they happen to be my favorite colors, black and gray. Returning to the line marking the proper distance, I turn to take my first throw. Homing in on the board, my focus centers on the bullseye. Since it doesn't feel right to throw the game, maybe I can end it fast by knocking out my opponents quickly. As I release my first dart, unexpected hands pressing on my hips make me jerk, sending my dart wide. It hits the board, just not where it matters.

"Let me help you get in the proper position," The asshole tells me. Great, now I need to burn my jeans too.

"I got it, thanks."

"Well, if that throw is anything to go by, I will have to respectfully disagree with you, darling." Darling, what the hell? I am no one's darling, and definitely not this guy's.

"No, really, I got it." My reply is given more sternly as I slip out of his grasp, but he seems unrelenting as he grabs me before I can get too far away. This time he pulls me back into him so my back is firmly against his chest. Shit—shit—shit, how the hell did you get yourself into this situation?

"I think you should let her go now, Max. She said she has it." Thank goodness Hyde realized what was happening because, besides Shelly, whose eyes are the size of saucers seeing his brazen behavior, no one else is paying any attention to us.

"I don't think you know what she has. So why don't you take your geeky ass back up to the bar before I escort you." Alright, this asshole just crossed a fucking line.

Spinning, I shove him away from me as I growl, "Why don't you?"

"Now, don't be like that, darling. I'm just trying to be neighborly."

"Don't need no neighbors, and I said I have it. Thank you."

"I like feisty bitches like you," he snatches out, grabbing my arm, and instantly I flash back to Travis, my room, and what he intended to do, causing my hands to tremble. Laughter erupting around me after Max makes this declaration has my heart dropping at the thought these people are no different from my pack was, but almost as fast, I hear someone else.

"I believe the lady told you she was good." Turning, I find the big guy Ness informed me is Denver, standing directly behind me. And it appears the laughing was not at my expense as one of the other contestants tries to pull a dart out of the wall.

"Down boy. I told Ed I would teach her what she needs to do."

"First, I am not your fucking boy. Second, teaching doesn't include touching. So take your hands off her before I remove them." Denver's voice drops lower. Since I don't know him well, I can't say this for sure, but I would almost say it was a warning.

"I'll help you, Shay," Hyde announces without removing his glare from the asshole. I know he may not be afraid of Hyde, but with Denver, he does seem to be…. Not afraid; I don't think this asshole has enough sense to be scared, maybe mindful. Yeah, mindful may better explain his reaction to the mammoth man standing behind me. Not to mention this big guy has another friend who is now watching the interaction between us. Max raises his hands as he backs towards a booth filled with several other men now on their feet.

My cheeks burn hot, knowing I am the center of attention once again. You can open that hole to hell anytime now, I silently say to the ceiling. When people slowly return to their own games, I chance a glance over at the table he retreated to, and for the second time in my life, I find the murderous intent of another sadistic prick watching me.

Episode Twenty-Four:
Winner, Winner

Foster

I KNOW WITH the way Ed currently has the bracket set up, we should not have to face off for quite a while, if at all. Here's hoping for the at-all path. When she tells Ed she doesn't know what to do, I roll my eyes, but when I hear who volunteers to help her, I want to storm over and demand anyone other than this prick mentor her, but if I intend to stick by my plan of not claiming Shay, then I need to let this go. Even if I think Max is a sleazy bastard.

What the hell is wrong with you, dipshit? We can't leave our mate with Max. He's lower than pond scum.

She's fine.

We know how bad he is to women. You and I have both seen the damage caused by his so-called love, so get your ass up and get over there before I make you.

Make me? Do you really think you have enough brass balls to make me do shit? Besides, furball, It's not like she's alone with him.

NO! Protect mate, and brass balls are better than blue balls. You blue-balled wonder.

What can he possibly do to her in a room full of people? The answer is nothing; he can't do shit.

Coward! Shadow has never acted like this before, and I hate being at odds with him. We have always been completely in sync with one another, but it seems this one issue may drive a wedge between us.

Pushing all thoughts of her aside, I turn my attention to my current challenger. Jim is a great guy, which is good since he isn't so great at darts. In fact, Ness could probably beat him, and she doesn't have the first damn clue about how to play this game. He does it because he likes to hang out with us, not because he cares about winning or losing. This makes me like him more, and because Jim is such a great guy, I think I might throw the game to him. The problem is the longer we play, I realize there is no damn way I will be able to because he can't seem to hit even one of the required numbers to win a round of cricket. He would have the game in the bag if three or six were the only numbers needed.

Someone begins arguing somewhere to my left, which in itself is not unusual during one of the tournaments. Someone is always claiming their opponent cheated or just being a sore loser. This is until I hear her raise her voice. Nope, I am not going to look. Nothing can make me look over there. This is not my problem.

Jim's last throw misses the board altogether, which has the entire crowd of people around us laughing as he takes a bow, but I'm not paying attention to the merriment around us since just before he released his dart, I heard Max call her a bitch. Snapping my head in their direction so I could see what the hell was going on resulted in my own dart getting stuck in the wall, and of course, my cousin found the wayward dart throw hilarious. I realize he is grabbing her, and she doesn't seem comfortable with his unwanted handling of her. Seeing him manhandling her like this has my wolf going crazy.

Calm down, Shadow! It's not often I use his name, but he is so enraged I know if I don't calm him down soon, he is going to force the shift against my will.

Protect mate. Protect Shay. Do it now, Foster! Before I can begin moving in her direction, Denver is there. His stance is clear.... Maximus will either relent or face him.

See, she's fine. Denver has it under control.

OUR Mate.... NOT his. We protect Shay, Not HIM!

And I've told you I don't want a mate.

Too damn bad because the Moon Goddess—Made a mistake in giving one to us because I have no intention of claiming her. Now let it go. Shadow slams the door closed on our connection for the first time ever. Making it much less noisy while I concentrate on the game, but at the same time, it's too quiet now.

*****

Shay

There are not too many things in my life that rattle me besides Travis and, apparently, now Max, so I am not ashamed to admit seeing the look in his eyes right now more than rattles me; it scares the shit out of me. My wolf, who senses my fear and his rage, begins to whimper. The irony of this situation is not lost on me since I ran from my pack to get away from a sadistic prick, only to end up in a town that has one who is as bad, if not worse, than the one I left behind.

"Do you need a minute, sweetie? I'm sorry I wasn't any more help. I have to admit he scares the shit out of me," Shelly softly tells me.

Denver must realize how uncomfortable I am; as a result, he storms over to where Shelly and I are standing. His focus is fully on the asshole he just sent scurrying back over to the booth in the corner, "Why don't we switch boards? You two take our board; we'll take yours." The rest of his statement is said loud enough to once again pull the attention of everyone in the bar, cue the red rosy cheeks I was just starting to get rid of. "That way, if the asshole over there feels the need to continue staring, we'll be the only ones he sees."

Seamus, who has been in the kitchen for most of the exchange, comes out to figure out what the ruckus is about. Like every other typical asshole in the world, Max refuses to let this go and decides to blow Denver a kiss. As I'm sure you can guess, this does not go over too well. Reaching up, I place my hand on Denver's arm, hoping to halt any further fighting since it's kind of my fault he's arguing with Max to begin with. The guy who came in with Denver moves to stand between the two men. If his glare is anything to go by, then I would have to say, there is no love lost between him and Max either.

"Aye, if you're not in the tourney and yer acting the maggot, you can leave me bar." Seamus's eyes are settled on Max.

"I was just trying to help the new girl until that big ass gorilla had to stick his nose where it didn't belong." When Seamus comes around the bar, Max stands up, telling the men with him they're leaving. I'm unsure if Seamus is some badass or what since Max doesn't argue with him. I admit it makes me feel safer being here. Shortly after they leave, the bar settles into a much more relaxed atmosphere allowing the tournament to resume. Round after round, I meet my opponents head-on, and each one walks away amazed they lost to me. Now that I have figured out how this works, I have no problem finding my next challenger or board I am slated to play on.

Holy shit, I actually made it to the final round, but my elation is short-lived as my heart jumps into my throat when I see who I am going up against; Foster. How is it possible that out of all the people in the tournament tonight, the final two are him and me? I am truly beginning to think the Goddess has it out for me. I must have a horrible soul to be this far down on her shit list.

"Alright everyone, it all comes down to this...." Several people drum their hands in anticipation of the announcement. "Newcomer Shay versus Foster," Ed's announcement amps up the already rowdy crowd. Why, oh why, did I not throw the last match? I could be safely tucked behind the bar serving drinks, but no, I had to throw two triple twenties and a double bullseye to win it. Someone next to me kept yelling I got a perfect finish. I just thought he meant I did good, but I guess it is the correct term for what I threw.

So that stupid perfect finish has me going against the one person I didn't want to face. Ed is making us each take a turn to see who can get closer to the bullseye; this will determine who throws first. I admit the term he used, Diddle in the Middle, has me giggling until Foster looks over at me. He probably thinks I'm crazy. I'm still amused when I make my throw which goes wide, and Foster takes the win. He advises he'll go first, which is kind of crazy since most people want to bat clean up, so to speak, not lead off. I know I am mixing my sports analogies but give a girl a break. I wasn't permitted to watch much television, so I only know so many things I can use as a reference here.

Walking up to collect the dart I threw, my hand brushes against his, making my wolf snap to full attention. Her happy, content sigh from the contact with our mate is short-lived when I jerk my hand away, mumbling a quick apology.

Round after round, we compete, and it all comes down to this. He is twenty-five points behind me, while I only need a double eighteen to end the game. The problem is I am so damn distracted being this close to him, especially since neither of us is speaking to the other; I can't seem to land it. My first shot hits a double one. My second shot is a single four. Closing my eyes, I know this is the last dart I will be throwing tonight because once he settled down, his game has been flawless. I have no doubt he is going to land the double eighteen he needs to end it on his next throw. Taking a deep breath, I let it out, home in on the space I need, and release my dart. It flies straight and true and sinks within the area I require. The entire bar goes crazy. People are throwing popcorn in the air. Several people rush up to yank me off my feet before they kiss my cheek. The entire affair is unnerving.

Finch, Ness, Denver, and his best friend, whom I have come to learn is Atlas, all surround me.

"You just accomplished the impossible; you dethroned the reigning champion," Finch yells as he drapes an arm around my shoulder.

"The reigning champion of darts?"

"No, the reigning champion of everything. Foster never loses. To anyone…. Ever." Ness and Atlas nod their heads as Denver grins at me. My eyes glance in his direction, but he is currently leaning on the bar, engrossed in a conversation with Mandy.

Episode Twenty-Five: Threw It

Foster

"*Y*OU THREW THAT game to her, didn't you?" Finch asks as we finish the frame for the building they contracted us to put up.

"I'll have you know I have never willingly thrown anything."

"Until last night when you gave the lovely and sexy as-hell Shay the win." Upon hearing him call her lovely Shadow growls, I admit to being pissed at the sexy comment.

"Didn't happen."

"Yeah, okay cuz, whatever you say." Finch retorts as he leaves to get the supplies we need to begin wiring the room.

You can tell Finch and Rom whatever you want, but you and I both know the truth.

Yeah, and what would that truth be, Furball?

You did throw it, blue-balled asshat. Shadow gloats.

I was just sick of playing. And my balls are the same color as the rest of my body.

Not true. You could have won the previous round. You gave it to our mate. And if they ain't blue yet, they are well on their way. Shriveling up to little prunes, they are, from lack of use.

Jesus Christ, I let a new person in town win a stupid dart game. Is he laughing at me? Who the hell knew a wolf could laugh, but I swear it sounds like this asshole is laughing at me.

Shut up, furball. Now he's laughing even harder.

The rest of the day drags by with either Finch or Shadow giving me shit about the dart game. I have never been so damn happy for a workday to come to an end.

"We still having the party this weekend?"

"What's this we shit?" I ask, finally seeing a way to get back at him for all the crap he gave me today.

"Don't get all salty. No one cares if you have a thing for the new girl. I mean, she is damn—"

"Sexy. Yeah, so you've said." I snap, not wanting to hear him say it again. I do plan on having the party this weekend, but I also need to follow up on a lead I have on Deacon. I'm not sure what this asshole is up to; whatever it is, I believe it involves another useless piece of shit, Max. If they are dealing with one another, nothing good can come of it for our pack.

If Deacon thinks he is going to bring Max into the pack, he has another damn thing coming. There is no way in hell I will allow it. I took out one tyrant. I will not have any issues doing it again.

My cell goes off, pulling me from my lingering thoughts of what our pack leader may be up to. When I remove it from my back pocket, I discover Ness's name on the screen. The only time Ness calls is when she is worried about me or wants something. Since she just saw me last night, I'm going to go with the latter. Turning the phone so Finch can see whose calling, I put it on speaker.

"Hello, Ness."

"Foss," the way she drags my name out, I know she wants something.

"What do you want, Ness?"

"Now, why would you go straight to me wanting something?"

"Intuition. So you wanna tell me what you want, or are we going to pretend like you're calling for any other reason?"

"Are you still sore that Shay beat you in darts last night?" Finch's chuckle does little to help my growing ire on this subject.

"I am NOT sore about shit."

"O. K. Grumpy, geez."

"Ness." I am beginning to lose my patience with her, and if she doesn't get around to asking me what she called for soon, she'll be asking a dead line because I am about thirty seconds from hanging up on her.

"Last night, you said you would teach Lindsey and me—"

"The answer is no, Ness. I'm not coming over to the bar tonight."

"Why not?"

"Because I worked all day, after getting home late last night, and I'm tired. Besides—" Before I finish this sentence, I think better of it, asking instead. "Am I on speaker?"

"Yeah, but it's cool. I haven't picked Lindsey up yet." Ordinarily, we tend to stick to other shifters, but Ness has always been friendly with none shifters. While Lindsey has been around for a long time, she's never acted any different around us, so either she knows and doesn't care like Seamus, or she's still clueless. No point in taking any chances though.

"I need to exercise Shadow. He's been a pain in my ass for a week now."

"Hmmm, right around the time Shay showed up," Finches eyebrows shoot up as he begins tapping the side of his mouth, hearing his sister's thoughts on the issue.

"Don't fucking start Ness. That girl has nothing to do with it."

"Umm-hmm." Before she can say anything else, I hang up. Finch lifts a finger to impart some of his own thoughts on the subject.

"That goes for you too, asshole." My cell alerts me to a new text. It's from Ness; it simply reads *Next Monday Stooges B there or B square,* although an image of a carpenter's square replaces the word. She has always found this hilarious for some unknown reason. She then sends me a kissy face emoji, to which I fire off a one-word response, "Maybe."

After dropping Finch off at aunt Clair's and promising her I'll be here for Thanksgiving dinner in a couple of weeks, I drive to my house. The second floor is the only one I haven't finished. I need to rip out the walls up there and completely rebuild everything. The plan is to put my bedroom up there along with a second bathroom. The main floor has two smaller rooms I can use whenever Foss or Ness crashes over here.

Dropping my gear, I strip and head out to let Shadow play. He's been romping around chasing small prey for close to an hour when we find ourselves towards the edge of our pack's land. This is when I notice another wolf lying on the outcrop of rocks by the edge of the stream. I don't believe I have ever seen this wolf before. Their fur is stark white against the surrounding backdrop of evergreens, further confirming this is not a wolf from my pack. At first, Shadow wants to investigate, but when I hold him back, he quickly changes his mind from wanting to examine to needing to claim.

Mate, Shadow declares

You don't know that, Shadow. I reply, forcing the shift so I can be in total control. Something about how the wolf is laying leads me to believe it is female, but I can't know that for certain, and I'm too far away to figure it out. Thankfully the wind is blowing towards the west, so while it carries their scent downstream, it also takes mine.

A sound from some place behind the other wolf has her scrambling to her feet. Her ears are perked and rotating, trying to ascertain where the noise came from. A few seconds later, she turns and rushes into the woods behind her, vanishing from my view.

After waiting to see if anyone else will show up, I allow Shadow to take over as we make our way back home. Once we get there, I grab a slice of cold pizza and a beer before pulling out some of the files I copied while in Deacon's office. There are a handful of invoices for materials we have never used on any job, and since I am one of the main supervisors, I know every piece of equipment, material, and supply we should have.

I still can't find anything to indicate why he's working with Max. Still, I know he is because I found a canceled check made out to Roman Transport which is Max's company, and a meeting with a person named Max was penciled into his schedule. He's the only Max in this town and all the surrounding communities, as far as I am aware. Finally, several of the supplies he purchased would better be utilized in the company Max runs, not ours. Now I just need to figure out why and confront the asshole. Unfortunately, this will have to be a problem for another day because I'm exhausted from our lack of sleep last night, the ten-hour day at work, and letting my wolf out for several hours. Tomorrow I need to get the rest of the supplies for the damn party Finch set up, and I still want to stain the rocking chair I have out on the porch.

Episode Twenty-Six: Investigation

Brady

TODAY IS THE first time I have been able to slip away all week without Travis or Coltan wanting to follow me. I had to tell them I was meeting a girl just so they wouldn't want to tag along. For whatever reason, Travis is hellbent on going everywhere with me. I don't know if maybe he made a mistake the morning after Shay went missing that allowed her to slip through our grasp, and now he is trying to cover it up or what. I hate to accuse him of something without proof; the problem is he is making himself look guilty as hell.

Arriving in Whitefish, my first stop is the bus station; if Travis happens to show up, I would rather he not hear what they say.

"Can I help you?"

"I was wondering if you could tell me if this girl came through here a couple of weeks ago?" I hand him the photo. The attendant studies it for a second before calling over a young woman.

"Hey, isn't this the girl who was in here counting dollar bills for her bus fare?" He asks, handing the photo to Liz, if the name embossed on the name badge is anything to go by.

"You should know, Jake, since you couldn't stop talking about her for the rest of the day," she laughs before looking like she just put her foot in her mouth since she has no idea who I am to the girl in the photo, nor have I told them why I am inquiring. She pulls her mouth back in an eek expression before saying, "Sorry. Is she your sister?"

"No, she is not my sister."

My pointed answer has her mumble, "Shit."

"She is also not my wife or girlfriend." Liz lets out an auditable sigh. "But she is a friend, and I am trying to find her. Do you happen to remember where she went?"

"I can't remember where she ended up going to, but I can tell you she originally wanted to get to Texas but didn't have enough money—"

"Wait. What?" Shay stole a million dollars. How in the hell did she not have enough money to pay for the fare to get her to Texas?

"Yeah, she wanted to get to Texas but didn't have enough money for the ticket, so she changed her mind and bought a ticket to…. Darn, I can't remember, sorry." Jake advises.

"Do you have to provide ID to purchase the ticket?" I asked, hopeful if they require ID, they may also keep records of where the purchaser is traveling to. This would be the best-case scenario cause then they could check their records and possibly give me the route she was traveling. Even if she did purchase a ticket, it doesn't mean she traveled to the destination on the ticket, nor does it mean Shay stayed there after she arrived.

"No, we don't require ID."

"So no record then of where she went to."

"Sorry," Liz responds. "I wish we could be of more help. Good luck. I hope you find your friend."

"Thanks," I huff in frustration. Now I know she left here by bus, not by truck. Unfortunately, this information means diddly squat since I don't know where she traveled. Taking the photo back, I tap the counter with it a couple times before lifting my hand in thanks before turning to leave.

"Oh my gosh, I remember," Jake yells, causing me to look at him over my shoulder. "She decided to travel to Colorado, or was it Utah? No, I'm fairly certain she went to Colorado. It was definitely one of those states in that vicinity." Great, so I have thousands of square miles to cover looking for a wolf who can disappear into the wilderness.

Leaving the bus station, I head over to the general store. It seems our friendly, helpful store owner, clerk, whatever he is, wasn't so helpful after all. Now I would like to know why. The exasperated look crossing his face when he sees who came through the door has to mirror my own since if this guy had not lied, half of our pack wouldn't have been searching in the opposite direction. When I walk in, I discover the clerk is busy putting stock out. He turns when the little bell over the door alerts him to a customer's presence. The bright smile covering his face when he first turns doesn't last long when he realizes I am the one standing here, resulting in the beaming grin to slide away just as quick.

"Are your little visits gonna become a weekly thin' now?" Leaning against the counter, I don't respond. "Well, I'll tell you the same thin' I told you last time you came in. The girl came in, got some food, and left with a trucker headin' east."

"Except we both know that's not true. She actually left by bus heading towards Colorado." His hand briefly falters before he returns to stocking the cans on the shelf.

"Well, I reckon she must have changed her mind."

"Yeah, see, I don't think she changed anything. Furthermore, I believe you already know that, sir."

"I don't care what ya think you know, young man. Cause I don't reckon you or your friend is worth spit."

"That sounds like a whole lot of hate, and here I thought we could be friends."

"I'd rather cuddle with a hornet." Okay, I'm starting to think this guy doesn't like us, but I haven't been as nice as I could have been to him, especially since Travis jacked this guy up by his shirt the last time we came here.

"Listen, I think we got off on the wrong foot," the guy looks at me like I'm a complete dumbass. "We had a lot of money come up missing the day Shay left. I don't care where she wants to live; I just want the money back. Those funds were slated to go to the hospital just south of here for research into a rare cancer that only affects kids. So with this in mind, sir, if you think of anything, I would appreciate any help you can offer."

I stand there waiting to see if this will loosen his lips any. When he continues to pretend like I am not here, I give up but not before saying, "Sorry to have bothered you."

Just as I am about to exit the store, he tells me, "If that money story and what those funds are for is real and if it is truly missin', then you might want to look at someone closer to home."

"Are you saying someone else stole the money?"

164

"I'm sayin that girl didn't take diddley. She was runnin from someone, not cause of takin' sumpin that didn't belong to her. If you wanna find it, I'm sayin' you should start by lookin' closer to home, son."

"Thank you. I will." It should piss me off that this guy lied to us since he caused us to lose a shitload of time, but I'm not. I can't say for sure if Shay took the money or not, but something he said rings true. Why would Shay take the money now? We treated her like shit her entire life; why wait until now? When she knew I would be taking on the role of Alpha soon. Common sense tells me if she was going to do something like that, it would have been long ago. Besides, I saw Shay in her room not even two hours before Travis raised the red flag about Shay and the missing money. She looked like she was getting ready for bed, not getting ready to steal a million dollars before taking off with it.

Then there's the fact that she didn't travel as far as she wanted, telling the guy at the bus station she didn't have enough money. None of this shit is adding up. Damn it to hell. Have we been chasing the wrong person this entire time? And if we have, if she didn't steal the money, then what happened to make her take off so abruptly?

Running back over to my car, I know Travis and a bunch of the others had plans today, so I'm hoping I can make it back in enough time to search a couple of rooms. I have a few people in mind who may know more than what they are telling us; I also know who is the first one on my list.

Episode Twenty-Seven: Luck of the Irish

Shay

YESTERDAY WAS A whirlwind of emotions that started with contentment, changed to excitement, morphed into anxiousness, disintegrated to fear, and ended with amazement. Yes, even with the rays of a new day, I am still amazed that I not only made it through my first day of work without any major catastrophes but also competed and won a dart tournament. The fact I also met some wonderful new people who I really liked is the icing on my cake. As terrified as I was to leave the only life I knew, I have to admit I am starting to love my life. Now I just need to find somewhere to live, and my world will be perfect.

Strolling down to the local convenience store, I find my favorite little old couple sitting there. Mr. Lisbon hands me a coffee and the newspaper while Mrs. Lisbon gives me a fresh-from-the-oven pumpkin muffin. Not really wanting to sit in the hotel room, I begin wandering around, hoping to find a park or some place I can sit to enjoy my breakfast while I peruse the paper.

I don't find a park; instead, I end up at Stooges, which is fine, and discover I arrived in the nick of time to help Seamus with the delivery. We make short work of putting away all the stock before I park myself at the bar.

"Ay, what are you lookin' for?"

"A place to live. I can't stay at the hotel much longer."

"Do ya have a preference?"

"Four walls and a ceiling." I laugh.

"I might be able to help," he tells me as he heads to the door. When I sit there staring at him, he barks. "You coming?"

"Oh, yeah, sorry." I hop off the stool and follow him. He takes me on a path that cuts through the woods behind the bar to the next block. Once there, he takes me into a cute little house that is nice, but I don't really see any of the Irish flare I figured I would find in his place. I like the house, but I am in awe when I walk into the kitchen. I love to cook; well, let me rephrase that I love to cook when I don't have to do it for two hundred hungry wolves and their cubs. I marvel at the stove, which is hands down the heart of this room.

"So?"

"So what?"

"What do you think?"

"Oh, your house is great, but this kitchen is amazing."

"Good, so do you want it?"

"Want what?"

"The house. Do you want the house?"

"Are you serious?" I clearly misunderstood Seamus. This isn't hard to believe since most of the time I don't have a clue what he's saying.

"Ay, I bought it while I was building me house."

My initial excitement dies away as quick since the reality is I know I can't afford whatever he wants to rent this place for. Allowing myself to look around at what could have been one more time, I hope my disappointment isn't evident in my response, "I don't think I can afford it."

"We can work out a fair price provided you do the upkeep. So?"

Trying to contain my excitement is damn near impossible. Yeah, it may be a tiny one-bedroom single-story, but if I say yes, it will be my one-bedroom single-story house, something I never dreamed I could have. I nod my head enthusiastically with a grin I imagine resembles an insane clown covering my face. I cannot believe I am this lucky to not only have this place but to have found people like Seamus and Hyde.

"Good, you can move yer stuff in today, Tichy." Seamus drove me to the hotel to gather everything I own, which sadly doesn't fill the back seat of his truck, let alone the bed. Thankfully he also said I can use all the furniture. As I am taking the last load in, I hear someone squeal.

"Do you live here, Shay?" I turn to see Ness sitting in her car at the curb. After a brief conversation, I invite her in. I have never had a space before where I could have a friend come over; hell, I never really had a friend to invite anywhere. Ness surprises me when she brings a bottle of wine for us to share together. We spend the rest of the afternoon laughing, chatting and drinking. I guess it's good that I'm not scheduled to work again until tomorrow. Seamus is such a great guy; he told me I didn't need to put a deposit down.

"So, do you have to work on Saturday?"

"In the afternoon, but I get off at five. Why?"

"Well, I want you to come to a party with Linds and me on Saturday."

"I don't know."

"What is there not to know? You like to have fun, right?" When I don't respond, she laughs, "You know what fun is, don't you?"

"The concept, yes," I tell her truthfully, but in a way, she might take it as a joke.

"Well then, lucky you met me 'cause I am an excellent teacher, not to mention my life is all about having fun. So have your cute little butt ready at six."

And this is how I find myself sitting in a chair, anxiously waiting for Ness to show up. After Ness left Wednesday night, I shifted and went out for a run; everything was going great until I thought I heard something in the woods behind me, but ultimately it was the feeling of being watched that sent me scrambling home. And I'm fairly certain I saw another wolf on the other side of the stream watching me from the woods. When nothing chased me, I chalked it up to nothing more than my nerves. I am aware there is a wolf pack close to Lake. I sensed it as soon as I arrived, but I have been careful not to cross onto their land.

The rest of the week went by without incident. Thursday night work was steady without the craziness of Tuesday. Last night Stooge's was busy, and luckily for me, the asshole Max nor the mate, who doesn't want anything to do with me, was nowhere to be seen.

Ness skids into my driveway two hours late. Climbing into her passenger seat, she mumbles her apology as she applies lipstick.

"I thought your friend was coming?"

"We're just gonna meet her there; she hates to be late, and I guess I might as well tell you this now if we're going to be friends. I'm late for everything. Mom said it started with my birth and never changed."

"No worries, I'm just along for the ride."

Ness makes a quick stop to grab some beer and wine. I offer to pay for some of it, but she refuses, stating that Lake's exalted dart champion does not pay for alcohol. The party was further away than I thought it would be. I hope nothing happens; otherwise, my only way home will be my wolf.

When we finally arrive at the house where the party is being hosted, I finally think to ask, "Soooo.... Who's the party for?"

"For? The party isn't for anyone. This has been a tradition for as long as I can remember. We all get together around this time of the year to have one last big blowout before we end up ass-deep in snow.

"Wow, what an awesome custom. Are you sure no one will mind that an outsider is interloping in your tradition?"

"No, why would you think anyone would care?" She gives me a grin while a slight chuckle escapes her.

Not feeling like explaining my previous life with all the gory details, I shake my head, "I just don't want to ruin any traditions."

"Don't be silly, Shay. Now come on, everyone's waiting for us. I just need to drop this stuff off in the kitchen."

We carry everything inside, and I am blown away by the place. The appearance is rustic, but you can definitely tell someone lovingly refinished everything in here. I am just getting ready to ask her who owns this house when the most amazing scent swirls around me. No, no-no-no, please, please don't tell me this house belongs to....

"Oh hey, Foss, I brought more beer." ...Foster. Shit, this is so damn bad.

Episode Twenty-Eight: Party

Foster

*M*ESS IS ALREADY on her way out to the bonfire, leaving Shay alone in my kitchen, looking entirely uncomfortable as she pushes the hair behind her ear. To say I am infuriated at my cousin for inviting her here without saying a word to me doesn't even begin to cover how pissed I am. She keeps her eyes directed at the ground, looking anywhere other than in my direction. I can feel Shadow stirs having her this close, and apparently, he likes her being in our house, making me snarl....

Don't get used to it, furball.

Yeah, because Goddess knows having our beautiful mate in the same house as us is the worse thing we could possibly want. He snaps sarcastically.

The room is filled with the wonderful scent she brings with her. I inhale deeply, letting my lungs fill with her wonderful aroma until I realize she is watching me. My irritation flares knowing she just caught me, and now I'm back to being pissed Ness brought her in the first place.

"What the hell are you doing here?"

"I—I'm sorry. I didn't—"

"Didn't what?" My clipped demand makes her jump, causing Shadow to growl his displeasure.

"Did I do something to piss you off?"

Yeah, Foster, did she? Shadow shouts.

"I didn't know you would be here."

"Ness invited me." Of course she did. I'm going to have to have a conversation with my cousin.

"Is that a problem?" She asks hesitantly.

"I generally like to know who's coming to my house."

"I didn't realize this was…. Or that she didn't…. I'm sorry, I can go." She begins quickly grabbing her stuff.

Don't let our mate leave. When I make no move to stop her, Shadow whines for a second before telling me.

I promise I won't try to claim her anymore. I will give up on it; just let us spend some time with her tonight…. I won't make fun of the color of your balls anymore either…. Please, Foster.

Shay practically runs out of the house. The screen door slams back, hitting the rocking chair I have sitting on the front porch, causing her to yell, "Sorry."

"Shay?" Ness yells from the bonfire. "Shay, where are you going?"

"I just remembered I have something I forgot to do." She replies as she sprints down the stairs and towards the driveway.

"At almost ten o'clock at night," Ness replies, running over to stop her. "I know that's not true. So why don't you tell me what's really going on." Shay's eyes are directed at the ground, but when she looks up, the hurt I find in the sea of blue

173

squeezes my heart. After several seconds, she looks from Ness over to me.

"Foster?" I have no desire to fight with my cousin tonight. I have no desire to have this conversation right now in front of everyone, especially in front of Shay; therefore, I remain quiet even as Shadow is screaming all kinds of obscenities at me.

"Ness, you should have asked your cousin's permission before you just brought me here." Ness snaps her gaze from Shay to me.

"Is that what this is about because I didn't ask you?"

"You should have asked me first."

"I have always brought my friends to the year-end party without asking you, and you've never had a problem before. Why are you being such an ass about this?" Because none of those girls are my mates, making it easy to keep my distance. But with Shay…. The only thing I can think about is how her lips would feel against mine. How amazing she smells; about burying my face in her long blonde hair while I hold her close to me. About running through the woods with her at my side. About how much I want to claim…. Being around Shay is dangerous for me; I just wish I could tell Ness these things. Maybe if I could, she would understand why I want to keep my distance.

Instead, I drop my gaze and mutter through clenched teeth, "You don't have to go. Do whatever you want, Ness. It's fine." Before walking away.

Hoping to erase the memory of the hurt I saw in her eyes and the sweet aroma that is all Shay, I walk over to sit next to Lindsey. Am I an asshole for doing this? Yes. Am I a jackass for yelling at her? Yes. Does she deserve to be treated like I've treated her since she arrived, simply because she is unlucky enough to be mated to me? No. I know I should have just had a conversation as soon as I realized who she was and set everything straight. Did I do this? No. Why? Because I am a complete and total selfish asshole jackass prick.

Lindsey, on the other hand, looks like she just won the lottery. I think this further confirms I don't deserve a mate, especially someone like Shay, nor do I deserve Lindsey's admiration. This is why the moon Goddess should have left me without a mate.

I glance over towards where they are standing. I can hear Ness over there trying to convince Shay to stay, assuring her I must have just had a bad day, and I'm a really great guy, not the total asshole she was just subjected to. Hearing my cousin defending me after my appalling actions makes me want to smack the shit out of myself.

I don't merit her confidence because I really am an asshole. I squeeze the bridge of my nose, trying to fend off the growing frustration with myself and the headache from Shadow's constant yelling. Shay is still looking over towards us when I reach down and grab Lindsey's cup to chug down whatever she has in here. I know if Shay decides to stay, I will not be able to resist being near her. I am finding it more difficult every time we are around each other.

Focusing my attention on anything other than her, hearing my cousin growling at me takes me by surprise.

"Why the hell did you treat her like that?" Looking up, I discover Ness looming over me, but Shay's gone. I jump to my feet when I realize I can no longer smell her.

*****

Shay

If I had any doubts that he didn't like me before tonight, it was just undeniably confirmed during this interaction. I watch as Foster walks over to the bonfire. He doesn't hesitate as he sits next to Lindsey on the swing before draping his arm behind her. Maybe she is the reason he hates me so much. Maybe they're dating, and he's afraid I will screw everything up for him. If this is the reason, I wish he would have told me so I could have assured him I had no desire to be mated with anyone. She can have him without worrying about any interference from me.

"Shay, I don't know what's going on with Foster tonight. The only thing I can think is that he had a bad day and unjustly took it out on you. It's pretty shitty of him, but please know he really is a good guy."

"I'm sure he is, but I should go all the same."

"Please stay, Shay. I feel awful. I convinced you to come and promised you'd have a great time, and then this happened." Glancing over towards where they are sitting, Foster is rubbing his nose like he has a headache. I hate the thought I am the one who is adding to his bad day, specifically since this is his house. When he takes Lindsey's drink, it further cements they must be in a relationship. I completely understand now why he has been acting as he has towards me. Having your mate appear out of the blue when you are already in a committed relationship has to be causing havoc for them. All wolves know how powerful the pull is to your fated mate. So I imagine Lindsey has to be terrified even though I'm sure Foster tries his best to assure her she has nothing to worry about. I just don't understand why Ness would subject her best friend to me. She should have never invited me out here. It is entirely possible he hasn't told anyone we're mates hoping to safeguard Lindsey's feelings. Much like I haven't said anything.

"Come back over to the fire with me. Have a drink; if you still want to go home, I'll take you, no questions asked. I promise." I take one last look at them, finding the hopeful expression covering Lindsey's face while Foster's is nothing short of irritation.

"You know it's been a long week for all of us. I think I am just going to go home."

"Let me grab my keys."

"That's not necessary. I can get home."

"Shay, do you have any idea how far we are?"

"Since I was in the car with you, I kind of have an idea," I try to smile and hope it doesn't look as fake as it feels.

"I'm not letting you walk. Let me tell everyone bye and grab my keys." I don't tell her I won't wait, but I also don't tell her I will. When she storms over to yell at Foster, I see an opportunity as I quietly slip away.

Marcelle Valentine

Also by *Marcelle Valentine*

Scarred by Fate Series
Ritual Nightmare
Breaking Purgatory
Fate's Ritual
Opposing Tartarus
Sacrificial Endings

The Ash Rock Series
Shadow's Moon Season One
Shadow's Moon Season Two
Shadow's Moon Season Three
Shadow's Moon Season Four

Arrival of the Four Horsemen Series
Death's Inquest
Pestilence's Judgment
War's Verdict
Coming Soon Famine's Punishment

Kindle Vella
Shadow's Moon Season One through Four
Seized by Sin
Silverwood Throne

Marcelle Valentine

Teaser

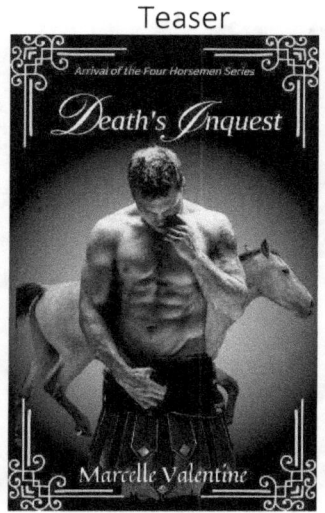

What do you do when you meet a fabled rider of the Apocalypse?

In my case, nurse him back to health, and hope like hell I can outrun him. Yet the whole outrunning him plan is proving to be more difficult than expected.

Has Avalon discovered the one being who can change everything, or will her fears come true? Grab your copy of Death's Inquest to follow Avalon's journey.

Marcelle Valentine

Acknowledgments

When I began this project, I figured it would be a short story, something I could use as a starting point on Kindle Vella. I never knew how much I would learn to love the characters or how much they would have to say. Currently, season two is underway on Kindle Vella, with season three coming in January and what I imagine is the fourth and final season will release in Spring 2023. Each season will come to Kindle and Kindle Unlimited 30 days after the season completes on Vella. If you decide you cannot wait to continue their story, jump over to Kindle Vella to catch up with the gang from the Ash Rock Series

My deepest heartfelt thanks go out to every reader who took a chance on an unknown author and gave this series a chance. I hope you got lost in their world, if even for a minute in time.

I could not have completed this series without the people who supported me, including my beta readers, my niece Ashley, my mom, and my daughter Melanie. Everything you each did to help me bring the series to life is something I could never say thank you enough. You each poured your time into this series to help me make it something worth reading.

I have several projects currently underway. With the first one in my horsemen series coming soon,

Thank you to my husband and everyone else in my family who have been my biggest cheerleaders. I love each and every one of you.

And finally, to every author that has ever put pen to paper, fingers to keyboard, whose work only inspired me more to follow this dream, I hope I do not disappoint.

Thank you
Marcelle

Marcelle Valentine

Newsletter

Consider visiting my website and signing up for my newsletter to receive updates on this series and all my future projects.

www. marcellevalentine.com

Please consider leaving a review on Amazon and Goodreads if you enjoyed the book. Any thoughts are appreciated and will only help me improve the story. Reviews also provide new readers with a way to find my books.

You can also follow me on social media

Facebook
Goodreads
Instagram
TikTok

Marcelle Valentine

About the Author

Marcelle Valentine has long been an admirer of creating worlds in which people can get lost. From a young age, her active imagination took her on epic journeys to faraway places where troubles and friendships abound. After discovering the intriguing world of Paranormal/Fantasy Romance, which stirred up memories of all those distant places and friends, her desire to write returned. She invites you to travel with her during these journeys and get lost in a world with friends, enemies, and lovers, all firmly rooted in the supernatural realm. Marcelle is the author of the Scarred by Fate Series and the episodic series Shadow's Moon. She lives in Ohio with her husband. She has two children, three grandchildren, and one lovable, lazy Great Dane.

Marcellevalentine.com

Facebook

Goodreads

Instagram

TikTok

www.ingramcontent.com/pod-product-compliance
Lightning Source LLC
Chambersburg PA
CBHW072236190626
46809CB00018B/2646